Contents

Contents

The Rosebush

"We're going to revisit your blood, run some extra tests since it's your third miscarriage in as many years, Mrs. Cozbi."

Susan stared into Dr. Tims' cold eyes, one hand gripping Chuck, the other the arm of the teak chair. "I thought it was because the fetus had too many chromosomes? You're saying there could be something wrong with me?"

Dr. Tims' face made a V shape, his gaze drifting towards Chuck. "Or him."

Chuck clutched Susan's tiny hand and began rubbing his fingertips over her knuckles. "What kind of tests, Doc? Is all of this really necessary? We'll just keep trying." Chuck said.

Dr. Tims took off his white coat, revealing a red bow tie against a baby-blue button-down shirt. "It's no harm, really. We'll run a few tests on the blood we already have and get the results back in the morning. If we don't find anything there, we'll see what we find in you, Mr. Cozbi."

Susan let go of Chuck's hand. "Please," she whispered.

On the car ride home, Chuck wiped Susan's tears with tissues he kept in the glove compartment. "I think it'll help you get through your grief if you talk to some-body, Sugar Bear."

Susan nodded, pressing her face against the window as she watched a woman cross the street, holding the hand of a child. "Maybe we can start thinking about adoption." Susan said.

"Maybe," Chuck replied, turning up the volume on the radio.

*

Susan sipped from a water bottle as she scrolled through her Google search. Dr. Tims' voice reverberat-ed in her mind, replaying the day's heartache. She pressed the bottle into her lips until it made a faint print on them. She stopped her thumb on the screen then tapped it on S*chedule Your Online Session Now.*

Susan turned to Chuck rolled over on his side. "Looks like we can get in with this guy, Dr. Randy Mont-gomery, tomorrow morning."

Chuck craned his neck to look at her. "We?"

"I'd like you there with me."

"Why?"

"I think we both have some things to talk about."

"Like what?" Chuck asked.

Susan closed her laptop and started to cry.

"Oh please don't cry, Susan."

Chuck moved closer and started kissing the top of her head. "Okay, I'll be there, Sugar Bear. If that's what you want, I'll be there with you. We can talk about everything."

*

Randy Montgomery wore a backward baseball hat and an adolescent scruff under his chin. The crunching sound of Chuck biting bacon muffled Randy's introduction to the session. "I'm not one to mince words. I know why you're here, so let's get to it. Tell me about your sex life."

Susan spilled her parsley drink, made religiously by Chuck, administered three times a day, an old family remedy for long life. Chuck noticed Randy staring at the green dribble on Susan's chin. "It's parsley drink, Doc. I grow the plant next to my rosebush. My grandpa showed me how. You see the parsley repels the beetles and attracts hoverflies. And then the hoverflies prey on aphids, one of the bugs that can quickly overtake our roses."

"So you're a rose farmer, are you?"

Chuck nodded, smiling at Susan. "Amongst other things. You see, a rose is only as beautiful as its ability to remain protected and alone."

Susan held the mute button on the computer and met Chuck's smile with a frown and straight lips. "Maybe this isn't the right guy."

Chuck picked up another piece of bacon. "Let's give him a chance, Sugar Bear."

Randy continued. "In all my years, well, two anyway, of counseling couples, the trouble couples have comes down to coupling."

"Coupling?" said Chuck.

Randy nodded. "Coupling."

3

A single tear struggled down Susan's cheek. She clicked the unmute button. "We received news of my third miscarriage yesterday. We just need somebody to talk it through with. That's all."

Chuck wiped his hands on his banana-patterned pajamas, then wrapped his arms around Susan. "It's been a rough patch, Randy. But I love this woman. I'd do anything for her. For us."

Randy flipped his hat forward. Bright blue stitching spelled *Beer Me* across it. "I'm sorry to hear that. But all the more reason for sex, I say. There's no blame here. How could there be? Something as terrible as a miscarriage. Nobody's responsible for that. It's just bad luck. Three times? Hell, real bad luck. Bad juju, maybe." Randy made a show of flexing his chest. "You need some new juju if you folks are tracking with me. And that starts with this." Randy pounded his fist into his open hand. The slapping sound echoed off Chuck and Susan's pasty white bedroom walls.

Chuck nodded, grabbed Susan's parsley drink, and titled it against her mouth. Her face made the usual squeamish expression. Even after five years of drinking the green goo, it never went down easily. Chuck set the glass onto the stained coffee table. He wiggled about in his chair, biting his fingernails, then, after an awkward silence, pointed his mouth into the laptop microphone. "Well, now that we're on this topic, can I be real for a minute here, Randy? Can I call you, Randy?"

"Sure thing," Randy replied.

Susan bent her neck to look at Chuck. He didn't notice her.

"There's not a day I'm not ready to paddle the pink canoe. To feed the caged kitty. Hell, I'll play the part of the three-minute wonder boy if I have to. But sometimes a man just feels like buttering his biscuit regardless if the oven's hot enough to get something growing. You know what I mean?"

Susan put her hands on her blood-moon cheeks, then inched her chair away from Chuck's, her face the expression of a deer in headlights.

Randy nodded in encouragement. "Okay, now we're getting somewhere. You people need some steam!" Randy stood and looked at a bikini-clad Ms. November hanging on the wall. He turned back to the couple. "Let me shift gears on you folks for a minute. From what I'm hearing, Susan is eager for kids so much so that Chuck, you feel overlooked and undercooked? Now Chuck, are you wanting kids at some stage, or would your prefer to just paddle around indefinitely on the white water?"

Susan's green parsley lips moved with trepidation. "It's no secret he doesn't want kids!"

"For God's sakes, Sugar Bear!" Chuck's voice boomed in Randy's earphones before Susan could say another word.

"Where the hell you get that idea from?"

Susan looked like a wilted rose, chin tucked into the top of her chest. "I remember what your grandfather said to us! I know what he tells you, what he thinks happened to his marriage because of kids! You're afraid of the same thing happening to us, aren't you, Chuck?"

"Yes. Get it out. Get it all out. This is good." Randy shouted.

Susan and Chuck sat with folded arms and straight faces. Randy made a note then proceeded. "Susan, what do you want out of motherhood?"

Arms dropping to her side, Susan whispered. "From the time I was a young girl, all I've wanted is somebody to love with my entire being, somebody who needed my care. A child would make our family complete."

"You hear that, Randy? This is exactly what I'm talking about. I've never been more than just a piece of a puzzle to her. Why can't I receive that love?" Chuck glared at Susan.

"I'll get to that, Chuck." Randy's baritone voice went bass deep.

Chuck stormed out of the room, slamming his hand on the wall on the way out.

Susan sobbed, looking at Chuck's empty chair. "I'm sorry, Randy. Maybe this wasn't the best idea."

Randy flipped his cap backward again. "Tell me, has he always been so adamant in not wanting any kids?"

Susan swiped her sleeve against her eyes and nose. "I'm just like his rose bush outside. To be protected. He's afraid he'll lose me otherwise. On our wedding day, his grandfather told us never to have kids, that having kids would only destroy the intimacy in our marriage."

The alarm on Randy's phone blared with the chorus from *Drop It Like It's Hot*. "Well, look at that. Our first session has come to an end. Let's get you scheduled in for your next one."

"I'm sorry. I don't think so." Susan closed the laptop before Randy could pick up his pen. The front door shutting made a gentle sound. Susan heard Chuck's car reversing out of the driveway. She watched him travel over the hill and out of view. A fresh parsley drink, a single rose, and a note rested on the entrance table.

I'm sorry, Sugar Bear. I'm with you. When I get back tonight, we'll talk about our favorite names. Don't forget to drink your parsley—all my love. Chuck.

A single tear ran down Susan's cheek and landed on Chuck's note. She smelled the red rose. The floral aroma buried the grassy scent from the parsley. She squeezed the bridge of her nose, then sipped the thick, green liquid. Her iPhone rang in her pocket. She set her drink back on the table and sat on a rarely used wicker chair. "Dr. Tims. Good morning."

"Mrs. Cozbi, we have some urgent news. I'm sorry we missed it earlier, but while reexamining your blood, we found an extensive amount of myristicin in it."

Susan's voice trembled. "What's that?"

"Myristicin is a common compound found in many herbs and spices, generally safe to consume for women trying to get pregnant. But the amount in your system is most definitely the cause of your miscarriages. Do you consume a large amount of nutmeg?"

Susan sipped on the parsley drink. "No."

"Carrots? Black pepper? Celery? Dill? Parsley?"

The green parsley drink spewed from Susan's mouth, painting the light brown door with a vomit color. "Parsley. I drink parsley three, sometimes four times a day."

"That's it! That's the cause of your miscarriages! How long have you been drinking parsley in such large quantities and why if you don't mind me asking?"

The iPhone dropped to the ground, shattering the face.

Susan picked up the phone.

"Mrs. Cozbi. You still there? Mrs. Cozbi?"

Susan began sobbing, and then she whispered, "Ever since I told Chuck I wanted kids."

Leaving for Love

John let go of the rusty door handle of his faded baby blue Chevy pickup. He shook Mr. Wilson's hand. "Mary's going to love it. When do we leave?"

"Next week, kid."

That night John's nervy stomach swirled as he stared at his bowl of spaghetti. He and Mary shared the last bit of a seven dollar bottle of Merlot in their only coffee cup.

"Babe, I've got exciting news." John said.

Mary's eyes lifted to meet his. "What is it?"

He took her hand and covered it with both of his. "You know I love you."

"What is it?"

He slipped his fingers into his pocket and placed Mr. Wilson's ring behind her ring-finger-knuckle, a near-perfect fit.

Mary's mouth opened big as a full moon, her bright teeth shining like stars against a sea of reddish-grey gums. "Where'd you get it?"

"Do you like it?"

"It's so different. So lovely. John, we can't afford this."

"You like it?"

"I love it." Mary sprung to her feet. "Yes! The answer is yes!"

John joined her, planting his bare feet on the cold kitchen floor.

John reached for her other hand. "I need to go away for a little while."

Mary slumped back down into the wooden chair. "What? Where?"

Eyes widening, John stepped around the table and kneeled before her. "There's treasure off the Ivory Coast. Mr. Wilson promised that I'll never need to work another job again! I'll finally be able to give you everything you've ever dreamed of!"

Mary pulled back her hands with a sharp, stabbing gaze. "The ocean?"

"It'll be a sacrifice, babe. For both of us. But it's the only way. I need to leave for us. For love."

Mary moved the ring up and down her finger until she finally pulled it off and placed it on the table. "It's Steven all over again! The same damn story! He said the same things you're saying now!"

The candlelight was dimming. The outside sounds of the night seemed to carry on out of tune.

"Your brother didn't know the ocean like I do, Mary."

Mary burst into tears. "I can't wait for you. You don't need to do this. I've never wanted anything more than your love."

John stood, pressing his hands into the table. "Look how hard I've worked for us. For you! And now finally an opportunity comes along, and this is how you act?

You know nothing about love!" John took the ring, slung it into his pocket, then stomped out the front door.

Trembling, Mary cried.

*

John never frequented the drinking holes. He was usually too tired or too busy working an extra job. For the past five years he'd been trying to give Mary what her parents couldn't, what her brother couldn't: security and safety, driven by his own ideas of what he thought she desired most.

Tonight he felt like drinking.

Larry's Pub was a mean place, locals only. Faint neon lights, hanging on by frayed wires, dangled in front of the entrance door. John ducked walking in, despite having plenty of room, afraid the sign might shock him if he got too close.

A string of four shoulder-to-shoulder men filled the only stools at the bar, leaving only space for seating around the main floor tables.

John sat with clenched fists, replaying the evening, with the feeling of an invisible rope tightening around his chest. Twenty minutes passed before he approached the barman.

The men sitting on bar stools held their drinks up, then threw them back into their throats. They raised their hands for another. When John edged closer, he heard a familiar voice.

Ricky Wilson was slurring his words, wobbling on his stool. On Ricky's right side, a man almost fell, bursting with laughter.

John thought about tapping Mr. Wilson on the shoulder to try to get a drink.

He refrained, for lack of courage, then curiosity. Inching closer, John pulled his big hat further over his eyes.

"I found another sucker in my field today. Good worker. Told him there's buried treasure near Ivory Coast, that if he comes with me, I'll make him rich."

One of the men shoved Ricky's shoulder, almost tipping him over like a salt shaker. "How the hell you get these kids to believe you, Rick?"

Ricky slapped the man on the chest, whispering, "I gave him a knock-off ring to prove there was loot!"

"No, you didn't!" One of the men shouted.

The barman topped the empty glasses. As quickly as the liquor settled, a new round fell into their throats, disappearing into the darkness of their gaping mouths.

"Said he needed that ring for his woman. I bet he's getting laid tonight! Better enjoy it! She might not be here when he gets back! If he makes it back!"

John's fists went rock stiff. He raised them to his chin, surveying a small opening on Ricky's left cheek. As John cocked his right fist, Ricky spoke again.

"He's strong enough, I tell you. He'll do good. By the time we've docked and got rid of the shipment, he'll be begging me to get off that boat. I'll be gone before he sees the light of day!"

"I don't know how you keep this up, Ricky. How you never get caught."

Ricky put his index finger over his lip then looked around the room, whispering, "It's not who you know. It's how much you're willing to pay who you know."

John walked away, collecting himself. When he returned, he stood peacock-chested, inhaling a deep breath. Heads lay flat on the countertop. Ricky was snoring as loud as the jukebox.

"Say, barman," John said. "Any idea what he's got in that shipment?"

The barman looked at John while collecting empty glasses. With shaky hands and nervy eyes, he whispered, "Cocaine."

*

When John returned home, the only thing left of Mary was her lavender perfume scent. Even the big suitcases, never used, were no longer underneath the bed. John fell onto the pillow, almost breaking his neck. Underneath the pillow was a framed photo with a note taped to the front.

This was the last time I saw my brother. Please don't go, John. All I've ever wanted was your love. I'm at my mom's. Mary.

John removed the note to examine the photo. Steven's smile was bright. He stood arm in arm with the rest of the crew in front of their boat. As John continued to study the photo, he gasped, stopping on a face in the back row. A shiver rolled down his spine. He squinted, feeling a bottoming out in his stomach.

Ricky Wilson stood behind the crew with a cigarette in his mouth, eyes cast toward the dark blue ocean.

Jamaican Johnny's Alien Adventure Tour

Paul opened the *Ya Mon Wireless,* sipping a Mai Tai and nibbling on a Saltfish Fritter. The azure blue pool water of the Montego Bay Hotel reflected the bright sun. A gentle nod and Paul's Dolce Gabbana shades slipped over his eyes in a perfect fit to the shape of his head.

Jamaican Johnny's Alien Adventure Tour: The Truth They Never Told You.

Paul slid the brochure in between Lisa and her selfie. "Seems right up your alley, Babe."

Lisa snapped her photo just in time, framing only her jade-Buddha necklace dangling above the cleavage of her recent double D expansion. "Five stars on Yelp! Over a thousand reviews. Guaranteed sighting." She turned to Paul. "Can we?"

Paul smiled, showing his set of moon-white teeth, too clean to be real. "Nothing like an extraterrestrial encounter to celebrate twenty years of marriage."

Paul rented a silver Land Rover the following day. Cyril, an old jewel-encrusted cornrow cat, offered emphatic advice. "Best tour on island. Some people call him a one-trick pony. But Johnny knows lotta shit 'bout aliens. Been playin' the same tune over. But it's a groove, mon. And a trip. Dig? Get swept up in his tune. And don't be using one of those superphones to find your way. Even them satellites can't pick up what's cookin' there. Follow this map. If you get lost, look for the black smoke. And tell Johnny I'm still firin' on this side."

The couple left their $800-a-night hotel room before the first rooster crow. Lisa stretched the map across the leather dashboard, trying not to make eye contact with an old woman knocking on her window at the red light. "What does she want? She's staring at my boobs, isn't she, Paul?"

Paul laughed. "I think I'm the only one who cares about silicone breasts in this part of the world, Babe."

The busy roads littered with vendors selling car-phone chargers, umbrellas, and chicken feet quickly turned into dirt-rutted ditches, eating the fat off-road tires of the Land Rover. Paul and Lisa's heads bumped the car roof every two minutes. Lisa tried holding her boobs, but they slipped out from under her palms, bringing a pain the plastic surgeon never warned about.

As she reached into her Versace handbag and tried to coat her lips with Bond No. 9, one of the small pre-anniversary day gifts from Paul, the road came to a dead end. Lisa hurled the lipstick back into the purse. "We're lost! I knew this alien tour was too good to be true."

Palm trees crisscrossed above the road. Slivers of sunlight slipped through the dried yellow-brown fronds. Foot off the gas, Paul looked sharp-eyed into the mirror.

"Cyril promised the map would get us there. Can you see any black smoke?"

"Who?"

"The concierge guy. Seemed to know the area. And Johnny too."

Lisa leaned forward in her seat. "What I wouldn't give to see a real-life alien. Just one encounter." She squeezed the Buddha in her fingertips.

Paul parked the car, smiled, then placed his hand on her thigh, rubbing it. His big black beard stopped at his brown Italian eyes. He looked at Lisa until her face softened. "How about a stallion?"

Lisa frowned. Paul placed his hand on her breast. "Let's leave the aliens and go back to the hotel room to find our own unidentified flying objects."

He leaned in. Lisa pulled away. "I bet we're close, Pauly. A little perseverance. Just like Dr. Alfred says."

"Dr. Alfred also says to get naked and have sex when you reach a dead end."

The phone unclipped from the charger. Paul held it high out the window. "Nothing."

"Oh, Pauly, you're the smartest person on planet earth. Surely you can figure out how to get us there?"

Paul got out of the car, climbed on the hood, and stretched his iPhone towards the sky. Nothing. As he was about to climb back in the driver's seat, he noticed a steady flow of black smoke sailing above the coconut trees. Lisa knocked her fist on the windscreen. She'd seen it too. "Look!"

They followed the smoke on foot. Paul squeezed Lisa's hand, the band of her ten-carat diamond ring digging into his skin.

Their wide eyes circled the jungly area. The green vines looked like snakes. Weeds and wildflowers painted a busy kaleidoscope of colors. Paul stopped. "Maybe take off your ring."

Lisa handed it to him with care. "You think they're interested in diamonds?"

"That's my year-end bonus. Better safe than sorry, Babe."

The trail ended at a burning stack of tires next to a pink jungle jeep.

They stared at the odd sight, mouths agape.

"It's the cyanide! Incinerates their skin. Just a little precaution in case of the reptilians." A muscular man with box braids appeared from behind the tires.

Paul extended his hand. "Are you Johnny?"

"That's right! Jamaican Johnny. What's cracking, my baby brother?" Johnny gripped Paul's clammy hand, let it go, then wiped his palm down his home-cut Capri shorts. "You Americans sweat like pigs, don't you? Them ETs don't drip an ounce. Got no glands like we do."

Paul put both hands in his pockets. "I'm glad we found you. We're here for the tour."

Johnny's bony finger pointed to the sky. "I wish I could help you, brother. But the blood moon sings tonight. All tours canceled. Me and my lady going to hum harmony, getting ready for a special visitation."

18

Lisa nudged Paul's shoulder, caught his eyes then rubbed her thumb on her fingers.

"I'll pay you twice your regular rate." Paul grabbed his wallet out of his back pocket and flashed a wad of hundred-dollar bills.

"Put that away! You think the ET's care about that paper-shit? If my babies weren't here, I'd kick your ass back to that fancy hotel."

From a clearing in the jungle, a petite, fair-skinned woman holding a baby on either hip settled in next to Johnny. She put a baby in his arms then walked towards Paul and Lisa. "Welcome! We're glad you've decided to spend your day with us."

"Told them to come back later, Minn. After the blood moon."

"I'm Mendy." Mendy smiled, then curled her palm around Johnny's shoulder. "Jirah needs his diaper changed. I'll take care of our guests."

Johnny set the baby on a mat on the dirt, then reached for Paul's hand. "I'm sorry I snapped at ya, my baby brother—much love to you. Much love." He wrapped his arms around Lisa, squeezed and kissed her cheek. "My lady, you have eyes for them. I can see it. Beautiful, my lady. Just beautiful."

Johnny disappeared with Jirah into the jungle.

Mendy sat on a white plastic chair, unbuttoned her shirt, and placed her breast into her baby's mouth. "He's special. I'm sure you can see that. People pay a lot of money to listen to him talk about aliens. He's an expert. They come here from all over the place."

"The aliens?" Lisa asked.

Mendy laughed. "Look, we're throwing Johnny a surprise party later today. It's his birthday in a week, but the blood moon means far more to him. We're dressing up in some damn near believable alien costumes. I've got extra. Three times the regular tour rate, and you can come. It'll kick the tour experience in the teeth, guaranteed."

Lisa shoved her hand into Paul's back pocket and grabbed his wallet. "What about the aliens? Think we'll see one? We read the reviews on Yelp."

Mendy moved her baby to the other nipple, eyeing the cash in Lisa's hand. "I'd bet my life on it."

Upon taking Mendy's advice, Paul and Lisa visited a nearby beach, swam, and drank rum cocktails out of coconut shells. They returned to the burning tire spot in the evening.

Four ground spotlights lit the lot. Mendy was wearing a white silk dress and holding a plate of chocolate truffles. "Welcome back." She handed Paul and Lisa a truffle each. "These accompany every tour. The most delicious snack you'll eat in Jamaica."

Lisa shoved the entire ball into her mouth, and then another. "Very good!"

Paul held the truffle to his nose, smelled then nibbled like a rabbit. "What's in these?"

Mendy had her head in a big duffle bag, pulling out a selection of costumes. "Any of these will do."

A neon-colored selection of leather garments sprawled across the dirt. Paul picked up a striped green and black costume with horns protruding from the head and a lizard tongue poking out of the mouth.

Mendy dusted it with her hand as Paul measured it against his body. "The Reptilian King. You'll pretend you're here to talk peace."

"Oh, a role-play of sorts? I'm very good at that!" Paul said, flashing a smile at Lisa who was struggling to fit a black and pink outfit over her chest.

Mendy helped Lisa tug the costume in place. "I'm not sure any creature has this shape."

Lisa laughed. "I hope they'll like them."

"The rest of the party is waiting for us in the tour cave. We'll hide in there until Johnny arrives, then see if we can surprise the hell out of him."

"What about your costume?" Paul asked.

Mendy curtsied. "You're looking at it. I'll be enjoying the visitation with Johnny."

Fire torches lit the path to the cave. The trunks of the trees had rune-like inscriptions in them, and their foliage hung in lobes.

Lisa saw repeating flashes of light in the red-black sheet of sky above. Every time she brushed through a long section of grass, it appeared to turn luminous. She squeezed Paul's hand then immediately let it go, surprised at how scaly it felt. "We're going to see them tonight. I can feel it."

When they arrived at the cave, Paul and Lisa greeted the other guests with a sheepish raise of their hands.

Lisa whispered. "They look so real, don't they? How are they all glowing like that?"

Paul rubbed his eyes, stepping closer, Lisa in tow. "Hi. I'm Paul, and this is my wife, Lisa. Thanks for letting us join the party tonight. We're ready to have fun!"

The group didn't say a word. Lisa thought she heard soft purring and droning. She tried to step in front of Paul, but he wouldn't let her.

"Alright, everybody, move to the back corners. Johnny's coming!" Mendy had a tray of truffles in her hands. She placed them on a large teak table dressed with a white silk cloth.

A deep baritone chant began just outside the cave.

"We know there ain't no smart in the truth they start, so let's listen to the speaking stars.

The forlorn gods keep raising their palms 'cause they think they gonna turn our heads into nods. But we done know the truth, and I'm here to show you I found the proof cause my lady and me tonight we groove."

Johnny's words formed a wave in front of Lisa's eyes. She rode the rhythmic trance, her head gravitating up and out from her body in a floating ecstasy. Paul wrapped his arms around her waist, careful not to make a sound.

Johnny's voice echoed in the cave. "I can smell all of you. Come out from your hiding place."

Mendy lit the center candle, pressed play on a psychedelic hits playlist on her iPhone, and the group of costumed aliens busted out from the corners in a frenzy.

Paul managed a muffled "Surprise." Lisa broke from his clutch, breasts popping out of her costume as she climbed on top of the table.

Deep slabs of bass and trippy shifting phases of synth delivered feelings of weightlessness.

Johnny raised his hands in the air, moving his head and hips with the gentle cadence of a hoverstar. When the first song finished he pushed his palms together in the shape of praying hands. Mendy lowered the volume of the music.

"Welcome, my friends." Johnny's eyes scanned the cave. "Greys, Hybrids, Nordics." He paused, staring at Paul. "Even the Reptilian King is here tonight. In a moment, we will soften our souls to hear from him."

The room cheered then quieted as Johnny raised his hands again. "My lady and I are but your servants to this world of lies and wicked men who seek to suppress your truth. Yet, this red night is the color of our hearts' devotion to you."

Standing bare-chested on the table, Lisa gazed at Paul with a look she hadn't had in twenty years. Johnny turned to Paul. "Reptilian King, enlighten our minds." The room burst into applause. Johnny stepped back and motioned for Paul to come forward. Paul drifted with the loud clapping and Lisa's eyes. He could see she was mouthing something. As Paul stepped closer to Johnny, he heard Lisa whisper. "Come for me, Reptilian King."

Paul's spine shivered with excitement.

Pushing his flat chest into the seams of the lizard costume, he stood on a chair. He spun his gaze around the room then settled it in Lisa's stare.

"My fellow extraterrestrials. The eons of time have given us more hardship than we were meant to withstand. Though abled with bodies of war and technology far beyond the pea-sized brains of our human kin, our destiny from here must be peace and love." The room exploded with joy. Johnny began break-dancing on the table, but all eyes remained on Paul, most notably Lisa's. "Thank-you." Paul raised his scaly hands. "So tonight, I will take one of you as my bride. As my prized possession of peace. We will be the sign of a unified alien race." Loud screaming echoed off the walls. Lisa moved closer to Paul, took his hand, and orbited her breasts with it. "Take me, Reptilian King."

Johnny grabbed Mendy, his forearms the size of war trumpets. He forced her in front of Paul's lizard tongue. "Humbly accept my offering, Reptilian King. May she serve as a bridge from my species to yours."

Paul placed his small, lizard hands on Johnny's broad shoulders. "You have done wonderful work, my son. Continue on this path with your woman." Paul turned Mendy face to face with Johnny. "Look after my son." Mendy smiled and titled her head.

Paul grabbed Lisa's hand then looked hard into Johny's eyes. "I will take this bare-chested black and pink species and usher in the peace we've all been searching for."

Johnny embraced Paul. "I will continue as you command, Reptilian King."

Paul acknowledged the rest of them, then pulled Lisa into the red-black night, her hands running wild, in and out of his alien skin.

Racing back to the Land Rover, Paul squeezed Lisa's hand. "Babe, how many truffles did you have? They spiked them."

"Where are we going, my king?" Lisa said, squeezing Paul's other hand.

Paul stopped. He stared into her bloodshot eyes. "My spaceship is waiting for us on the other side of the island. We must move quickly."

Midnight Sky

A stack of mail lay neatly piled on the dining room table. Picking up the top envelope, I heard a thud from the bedroom.

"Kayla? You okay, baby?"

Two open suitcases lay on the bed. My hands began to shake just as they usually did whenever I felt anxious.

"What's going on?" I turned nervously towards the bathroom.

Kayla shoved past me as she stormed towards her dresser, her hair wet, her cheeks red. "You knew this day was coming, Franky. You damn well knew it!"

"What are you talking about?"

She picked up her hairdryer and pointed it towards the living room. "That's three years of unpaid bills on that table! Three years of cleaning horse shit for that goddamn crook!"

I stepped closer, her back to me. I put my hand on her bare shoulder. The touch of her warm skin helped settle my shaking. "Give me two months. Please, baby. I've found a way. I promise. You got to trust me. I'm going to get us everything. Everything we've ever dreamed of."

She dipped her head and began to cry. "How long have you been saying that?"

"Oh, Kayla, please."

Lifting her gaze, she looked at me in the mirror. "You've run out of raises, and you know he'll never give you a bonus or that damn promotion he's promised you a hundred times."

"I've found a way. Something big. Bigger than all that." I squeezed her shoulder. "You need to trust me. Please, Kayla."

"You've got a month, Franky. Not a day longer." She brushed my hand away.

I wrapped my arms around her small body. She felt lifeless in my grip.

*

I arrived at the stables around 5 AM, only a few minutes before Danny. I waited for him at the run-in door, flashlight in hand.

When I saw his red Datsun pull into the parking lot, I shone the light on him.

He was humming as he approached.

"Danny, it's me," I whispered.

He stopped and lowered his head below the light. "Well, well, look what the cat dragged in! I never thought I'd see you in here this early, kid! Your girl finally kicked you out?"

I clutched his wrist. "You see anyone in the parking lot?" I shone the light behind him.

"Easy now, Scully. What's got you going all X-files on me?"

"I want in."

Danny grabbed the flashlight. He pointed it behind me and then into my eyes. "I don't believe you."

I put my hand on the flashlight, forcing the beam to the ground. Danny's eyes were bloodshot and the usual green of each iris appeared grey. He looked much older than fifty-five, his cracked, weathered face and nose hair dangling into his unkempt mustache.

"I'm telling the truth. Kayla's going to leave me if I don't do something. Something big."

"Who'd you tell?" His eyes widened.

"Nobody. Just you. I swear."

"You tell her?"

"No. Nobody."

"Once you're in, there's no going back."

"I know."

"How much you got?"

Danny reached for my hand and led me into the stable. "Never mind. We'll get to the details later."

We hurried to the back where the new horses were. "That's her right there." He said, pointing at Habiba, the mare Mr. Shariz had just acquired from the Persian Gulf.

"She's too young," I said.

Danny shone the light into my eyes. "Are you in, or are you out?"

"But…"

"We can't take any chances, kid. We got to be sure."

"How do you know she can run?"

29

Smiling, Danny put his hand on my shoulder. "You ever seen a horse from the Middle East that can't run? Take a look at who she'll be up against." He pulled out a racing sheet from his pocket.

"The end of this month?" I turned my gaze from Habiba and noticed Danny's wide grin. The sun was a glowing speck behind him. "That only gives us two weeks!"

"I ain't forcing you to do nothing, kid." Danny spat into his calloused hand, then extended it towards me. "You in or you out?"

I looked at the sheet again. I knew every horse, none of which had ever come close to winning a race, not even a small, private one like Mr. Shariz's quarterly bonanza. Handing the sheet back to Danny, I turned to view Habiba. The way the morning light rested on her white forelocks, she looked angelic.

"I'm in," I said, spitting into my hand.

*

Mr. Shariz hosted a private horse event every quarter. It was his primary method of moving the horses he had trouble selling. The evening would start with guests and their kids petting, feeding, and trotting the horses. Then, Danny and I would take some of the thoroughbreds and make them jump over boxes and through rings of fire. The highlight of the night was the race. The track we built was a small, serviceable, six lanes reserved for the horses we wanted to sell quickly. Shariz put up his own money for the house and took bets upwards of a hundred thousand dollars. Betters went in blind, guided only by the two- to three-sentence profiles I'd write for each runner.

We'd sit down with Shariz the day before the bonanza and go over the odds, a mere formality. Shariz only balked at our recommendations when the odds we set were too high. But we never lost him a dime.

*

"Washable. Non-toxic. Buy a few varieties of black and at least six gallons worth. You got that, Franky?"

Danny had me stop at the hardware store after work. We tested the paint on a similarly colored horse to Habiba the following morning, spraying a small part of the animal's underbelly.

"That's the one, right there."

"This one?" I pointed to the second streak I'd painted.

"Yeah, don't you think?"

"Midnight Sky." I nodded. "It looks sharp. No one will ever know."

"That's what we'll call her!" Danny smiled. "Midnight Sky!"

"So how exactly are we gonna get her on the card?" It was the question I'd been thinking about since shaking Danny's hand.

"That's the easiest part! You know Shariz can't keep track of his horses. And if he asks we'll tell him it's a sickly mare we've had for a while now."

*

"The standard lineup, boss. Six ready to go!" Danny snatched the sheet from me, framing it on the table for Mr. Shariz.

Shariz mouthed each horse's name using his index finger to follow the words of the profile descriptions, then the odds.

He stopped on the last name on the card. "Midnight Sky? I don't recall this horse."

He continued reading while I glanced nervously at Danny. "Thirty-five to one! What kind of odds are these!?"

"It's a sucker bet, boss. Remember that sick stallion a while back? The one we couldn't move."

"Sugar Boy," I added.

"Yeah, that's him. We gave him twenty-to-one odds that day. Remember what happened?"

Shariz continued studying the card, and then he lifted his head. "This is almost double those odds."

"Sugar Boy got all the attention that night with five buyers in a bidding war."

I couldn't look at Danny as he spoke. His voice had an unwavering confidence.

Shariz returned to eyeing the card.

"We've had this mare for over a year now, Mr. Shariz, and we suspect she's got laminitis." I kept my shaking hands below the table as I spoke, looking directly at Mr. Shariz.

"Laminitis? How the hell did that happen?" Shariz lifted his gaze.

"We'll move her, boss. Don't give it another thought." Danny reached for the racing sheet, tugging it from Mr. Shariz's grasp.

"Don't tell me what to think." Mr. Shariz yanked the sheet from Danny's fingertips, then turned it over and placed it on the table. There was a short silence. Shariz took a deep breath and began drumming his finger. "If this horse doesn't sell on Saturday night, don't come back to work on Monday. You hear me? The both of you."

Shariz walked out the office. We watched through the small, square windows, not speaking until we saw him get into his black Lexus and drive away.

"Seems extra angry today." I said.

"Who the hell does he think he is? You really think he can run this place without us?"

"You certain she's going to win?" I asked, my hands still shaking.

Danny picked up the card and threw it across the table like a frisbee. "You kidding me? She's gonna blow them by, Franky Boy."

Smiling, Danny stepped closer. "How much did you end up getting?"

"Almost twenty thousand." I said.

"That's all?"

"I tapped everything: retirement accounts, savings. Even got a loan from my parents."

"What about that guitar?"

"Which one?"

"That old, expensive one you told me about."

"The 1970 Les Paul?"

"Yeah, that's the one. Bring it with you on Saturday morning."

"Why?"

"Well, it'll give you another five grand to throw in the hat. That's what it's worth, right?"

"Yeah. At least five grand. My grandpa gave that guitar to me."

Danny squeezed the bony part of my shoulder. "Come Saturday night, you'll be able to buy ten of those!"

I stepped away from him. "I'll think about it. Who's your guy anyway?"

"Remember my buddy, Laron?"

"That man with the cane?"

Danny nodded. "We'll give him the cash on Saturday morning, just like we discussed. Throw in the guitar, and I'll tell him to add another five grand for you."

"And he's still okay with just ten percent?"

"He better be!" Danny laughed. "He's going to make seventy grand from your little stash alone! Never mind what I put in!"

I wanted to ask Danny how much he had riding on Midnight Sky. Twenty thousand dollars felt like a lifetime of money to me. I wondered if I'd ever see Kayla again if I lost it.

"And then what?" I felt nervous asking the question.

"What do you mean?" Danny's eyes narrowed.

"How do we get the winnings?"

He slapped my back, smiling. "Relax, Franky Boy. I'll get you your money when it's time. When it's safe."

I took a deep breath, fighting the urge to get a straight answer.

Danny clapped his hands. "I'll see you bright and early. It's payday tomorrow, Franky."

He looked me dead in the eyes. "Have faith. We're finally gonna get what's ours."

*

I grabbed Kayla's hand before turning off the light for bed. "It's happening tomorrow."

She sat up. "What?"

"My big score."

"You said two months?"

"I know."

Kayla smacked my thigh. "After the bonanza?"

I didn't look at her.

"Are you going to tell me? Is it a bonus? How much?"

I reached for the bedside light and pulled on the string. "I'll tell you once I get it. It's best to leave it at that."

"Damn you, Franky. Now I won't be able to sleep."

"I love you," I whispered, then kissed her.

"Please, Franky, you got to tell me."

Letting go of Kayla's hand, I spoke louder. "You need to trust me."

"Fine, can you at least tell me if I'll be able to buy that rug I love so much? The one at Sally's."

I smiled. "You'll be able to buy ten of those."

"Oh, Franky," Kayla pressed her body against mine and kissed me on the lips. "I love you."

"I love you too," I whispered, then turned over and closed my eyes.

*

I woke before my 5 AM alarm sounded, not hungry or interested in my usual cup of coffee. I changed, opened the safe, and counted my money for the fifth time. I tip-toed into the bedroom, removing my guitar from under the bed, making sure not to disturb Kayla. Before getting into my 97 Corolla, I scanned the neighborhood. I threw the money bag onto the passenger seat, set the guitar on the backseat, and rescanned the empty streets. I drove to work five miles below the suggested speed limit and made sure to come to a complete stop at every stop sign.

Danny had just finished applying the final coat of midnight sky to Habiba when I walked up. "That paint weatherproof?"

He dropped the spray can and stepped backward with a fast, surprised motion. "Damn, Franky. You about gave me a heart attack."

"Sorry, I thought you heard me coming." I looked up at the sky. It was still dark. I could feel the moisture in the air. "They say it's gonna rain today. Might not clear up before the race."

Making sure to paint even her underbelly, Danny reached his arm as far as he could, touching every part of Habiba. "Doesn't she look good, kid?" He stepped away from her, setting the can down.

I could hardly tell what color she was in the dim light.

"Did you hear me?" I asked.

Slamming his hand into a hay bale, Danny shouted, "You think I'm a fool? You don't know me, do you?"

My hands began to shake. I bent over, picked up the hay bale, and set it back on the stack.

"I'm sorry, Franky," Danny said with a much softer tone, "I didn't mean to yell at you like that. I'm just feeling a little nervous, that's all." He turned to look at Habiba again. "Of course, she's weatherproof. Ain't a hurricane going to take a speck of paint off her."

I'd never seen Danny snap like that in my three years of working with him. My hands were still shaking. I pushed them into my pockets and curled my fingers into tight fists.

"Where's the cash, kid? And what did you decide about that guitar?" Danny's tone firmed up.

"Now?" I said, turning my gaze to the parking lot.

"Laron's going to be here any second."

We walked side by side towards my car. Danny slung his arm around me, squeezing. He kissed my head as I put my key into the door. "You ready for the greatest day of your life, kid?"

I handed him the bag of money and guitar and watched him set them in the back seat of his Datsun. "Laron's got a spare key. He's going to trade out cars with me. I don't want Shariz looking for me once we've got the score."

I looked nervously at my Corolla. "Should I get rid of mine?"

"Nah, you weren't the one who put Laron on the guest list. Shariz will have no reason to think you're involved."

Danny locked his car. As we returned to the stable, I looked up at him, slowing my pace. "So how am I going to get my winnings?"

"Damn you, kid! I ought to cut you out of this deal right now." Driving his index finger into my chest, he shouted. "Are you going to trust me or not?"

I forced my hands into my pockets. As I tried to move a little faster to get ahead of Danny, we were both blinded by the headlights of a car speeding into the parking lot. We lifted our arms, shielding our vision.

"It's Shariz," I whispered.

"Don't act suspicious, kid. Walk slow."

We pretended not to see or hear Mr. Shariz and continued on back towards the stables.

A car door slammed. "Hey! You two!"

I stopped. Danny kept walking.

"Keep walking, kid," Danny whispered.

"I need help! Come here!"

I turned back, jogging towards Mr. Shariz.

"Danny gone deaf?"

"No, boss, he had to get to the feeders." Danny was out of sight.

"He's got to make sure Ginny doesn't take more than his fair share again."

Shariz opened the trunk of his Land Rover, groaning. "You know the drill, kid."

38

Sprawled across his folded leather seats were flower bouquets, beer and wine, folding tables, and a box of handwritten name cards for every guest.

"On it, boss."

I hurried the first load into my arms, then walked briskly ahead of Shariz towards the stables.

"Pretend you're hassling with the feeders," I whispered as I set the first load beside Danny.

*

"This will help out with the nerves, kid. Or maybe make it worse."

I took the cigarette from Danny. He handed me his lighter but quickly snatched it back after watching me on a few attempts. "Damn, kid, you're shaking worse than a California quake!"

"I didn't know you smoked, Franky." Shariz came thudding down the stairs.

Coughing, I managed. "Only once in a while, boss."

Mr. Shariz walked to the railing and viewed the grounds with his hands in his Tom Ford suit pockets. Turning to where Danny was sitting on a makeshift bench of two-by-fours, he picked up the carton of cigarettes. "All the horses ready to go, I presume? No complications?"

"It's going to be our best bonanza yet, boss." Danny flicked his lighter, then positioned the flame under the cigarette in Shariz's mouth.

"I haven't forgotten about that horse."

I inhaled too long and began coughing uncontrollably.

"Jesus, kid. Put that thing out." Shariz reached for my cigarette.

"I'm okay," I managed.

"She doesn't sell, and you're gone. The both of you."

"Oh, she's gonna sell, boss. I'm not worried about that one bit." Danny smiled, stubbing his cigarette under his foot.

"For your sakes, I hope you're right." Shariz returned up the stairs.

"You think he'd really fire us?" I whispered.

Danny set his hand on my shoulder. "Who cares, kid?"

He started to chuckle. "She's going to sell alright. Right after we've made out like bandits."

*

The bonanza moved along as nicely as any of the ones prior. As Danny and I lined up the horses for the final event, I kept inspecting Midnight Sky for any blemishes on her coat.

Danny brushed me away from her. "She's fine, kid. Get the other ones ready, will you?"

Steering the horses into their lanes, I looked into the crowd. The grounds were swarming with mostly high-profile businessmen and women and a few spouses and children who'd tagged along.

I felt a sharp jolt of anxiety when I spotted Kayla in a beautiful red dress and wearing a white sun hat. When she saw that I'd seen her, she waved and blew me a kiss.

"What's she doing here?" I mumbled.

"I invited her, kid. Thought it'd be a nice surprise. Told her not to tell you." Danny said, grinning.

"What for?" I snapped. "I thought the plan was for us to bust out of here as soon as the race ends."

"You're going to stay back and stall Shariz. Make it look like you had nothing to do with anything. Buy me time."

My hands began shaking furiously. I grabbed the top of the starting gate, leaning over.

"Get away from there," Danny pulled me off the gate.

I lost my balance, falling onto the muddy ground. "Why you only telling me this now?" I shouted, standing and stepping closer to Danny. "You know I can't pull this off by myself!"

Danny set his hand on my chest, "You got to trust me, Franky. I knew you wouldn't agree if I told you any earlier." He turned to Midnight Sky and began rubbing her head. "We've come this far, kid. I know you can do it."

"Ladies and gentlemen, are you ready for our main event!?" Shariz's voice boomed over the loudspeaker.

The crowd clapped and shouted.

"Which of these fine horses will you be taking home tonight?" Shariz looked over towards us, nodding.

Danny and I gave each horse a final check and nudged them forward. As I pushed Midnight Sky into the bright lights, I felt the rain hit my skin. Her black coat glistened. The crowd grew quiet as Shariz pointed his gun to the sky. Danny gripped the starting gate lever, smiling at me with an untrained confidence.

Bang.

A cloud of shining dust and rain obscured my vision. Hooves beating like drums into the earth overpowered the noise of the crowd. I turned to where Danny had been standing at the race lever. He was gone.

"Rounding the corner in the lead position is..." Shariz paused, then continued with a flatness in his voice, "Midnight Sky."

I stepped out onto the track and looked towards the finish line. No horse was going to catch her.

"Danny!" I shouted over the thundering noise of the crowd and hooves. "Danny, where the hell are you!?"

"And the winner is..."

The crowd cheered. Shariz dropped the microphone and pointed his finger at me, thrusting it multiple times. He left the announcement table, sprinting down the stairs towards the betting booth. The crowd blocked his way forward. He began to shove people out of his way, some of the men pushing back, refusing to step out of line.

"Danny!" I shouted, turning to the stable, forgetting to coral the horses at the finish line. As I sprinted out of the stables, I saw Danny and Laron getting into a black Toyota pickup. I chased them as they raced from the parking lot onto the highway.

Returning to the stables, I saw Kayla.

"There you are, Franky." Kayla wrapped her arms around my neck, kissing the back of my head.

I stood, searching for something to say.

"Are you ready to go rug shopping?" She whispered in my ear.

"What time do they close?" I said softly.

"Oh, Franky." She spun me around, pressing her lips tightly against mine.

I nudged her away when I heard fast, heavy footsteps.

"Where's that damn thief!? Don't tell me you're a part of this, kid!"

"A part of what?" I managed, sliding my shaking hands into my pockets.

"He set this whole thing up, didn't he? I know he did!" Shariz stepped closer. I could feel the warmth of his breath.

I took a step back, my gaze locked on his blue bowtie.

"Say something, god damn it!" Shariz jammed his finger into my chest.

"It was his guest. He put a hundred thousand on Midnight Sky. Took everything in the kitty tonight, but do you really think I'm going to pay the rest?"

Kayla stepped in front of me, buffering Mr. Shariz. "Franky said you're finally giving him what he deserves."

Shariz stared into Kayla's fiery green eyes. He said nothing before turning to me again.

"You're fired. Get the hell out of here!"

In the parking lot, Kayla grabbed my hand. "Where's the money, babe?"

I looked ahead and saw the skid marks made by the black Toyota pickup.

"Do you have it?" She asked again, speaking louder.

"Yes," I said, my hand shaking in hers like a feather caught in a gust.

Tom's Antique Shop

Robert Snow pounded his fist against his bedroom door. "Let me in, you selfish bitch!"

"You're drunk! You need help!"

Jacob winced as he heard his mother's scream. He cracked his door and watched his father retreat to the sofa in the living room.

The following morning, in the dark, Jeanie Snow sat at her study desk with a pen and a thick folder of documents. She heard Jake's gentle footsteps, then looked at him. Her eyes were red, and her cheeks sagged. "We're getting a divorce, Jake. I can't do it anymore."

Jacob didn't eat breakfast. He dressed for school, then walked two miles instead of catching a ride with his mother. Before the first bell, he cornered classmate Susie White. Rumors ran through town about the Whites. Nobody knew exactly how Steve White, a former drug dealer, had magically turned into a squeaky-clean, church-on-Sundays, family-van kind of man.

Jake waited until Suzy was alone at her locker. "Suzy, I got to know. How'd your dad do it? My mom's filing for divorce."

Suzy grabbed Jake by the collar and looked at him with a dead stare. "You got to get a mirror from Tom's Antique Shop. Do whatever it takes."

"What?"

Suzy let go of Jake, closed her locker, and walked away.

*

A week later, on his first day on the job, Jake moved a wet rag with care across the dark tinted window of Tom's Antique Shop.

"You make sure your elbows don't smudge where you wipe. And once that soapy water gets too grimy, you clean the bucket out. I want my customers seeing their beautiful mugs on their way out of here. You hear me, Jake?"

Jake turned around to look at Tom, who was sitting behind a desk piled with crap on it. "I'll do my best."

Jake went tiptoed and increased his hand speed, occasionally looking back at the shop's aisles, a picture of a giant ridgeback sitting on a sandy beach, a medieval-looking chair, and the door of a 1935 F35 Oldsmobile.

Tom rose from his chair, smiling as he walked over, watching Jake stretch his lanky arms, touching the top of the glass without the help of a ladder. "Good thing you're as long as a spruce."

Showing a full set of white teeth in the window, Tom used his pinky to pick a piece of meat from his molars.

"I got a meeting with a customer around noon today. Keep an eye on the place for me. You'll take your lunch after that."

Just before noon, town mechanic, Rudy Greer, walked in, greased to his ears. Tom greeted Rudy with an excited tone. "You ready for the encounter of a life-time, Rudy!?"

Rudy stared at his shoes, mumbled, and followed Tom to the back room. Thirty minutes later, the same sunken mechanic screamed into the hallway, hands touching the ceiling, legs bouncing up and down like pogo sticks. "It's been there all along! Everything I've ever wanted!" Jake watched Rudy stare at himself in the shop window. Rudy turned back to the register and handed Tom a stack of hundred-dollar bills. Shaking Rudy's hand, Tom gave him a mirror, and then Rudy left.

Heart thudding, Jake said, "Must be one helluva mir-ror, Uncle Tom."

Tom set the stack of cash in the till and grinned. "What my mirrors give to people is worth more than all the money in this world." He looked up at Jake. "I'd be lying if I said the extra cash isn't nice, too. To tell the truth, I'm not sure if I'd be able to stay open without selling these mirrors."

Jake dragged a cloth against a dusty nightstand. "How much are they?"

"Six months work for you."

Jake dropped his elbows on Tom's counter. The boy's eyes had dark lines underneath them, heavy and sad-looking. He straightened, then stuck out his palm. "Six months. You have my word."

Tom laughed. "You don't need a mirror. You're too young to be tainted by the cruelties of this life."

Jake's hand sunk, and then his head. He looked at a pile of gun magazines. His voice faltered. "It's for my dad."

Tom leaned over and squeezed Jake's shoulder. "I'll tell you what. You get your dad in here to come see me, and we have a deal."

The bright afternoon sun knifed through the tinted shop windows. Jake blocked the side of his face with his hand. He put his other hand in Tom's small palm and shook it until the glint in both their eyes faded with the ringing chimes.

*

That night Jake lay in his bed staring at the ceiling. A screeching sound made him jump out of bed moments before falling asleep.

Robert Snow thumped his fists against the front door and rattled the gate, shouting. "Open the door, Jeanie!"

The keys fell out of Jake's hands. "Take it easy, Dad. I'm here. Just a second."

Rob stumbled forward with outstretched arms, falling into Jake's chest. Jake held his breath as Rob slouched, the stench of alcohol souring the scent of Jean's fresh-picked roses. "Where's that bitch?"

Jake walked Rob to the living room, then dropped him on the long sofa. "Dad, I got something I want to ask you."

Rob kicked off his shoes, adjusted the pillow, then craned his head. Eyes crisscrossing, Rob slurred his words. "What is it?"

"I want you to come with me to Uncle Tom's Antique Shop and look into one of his mirrors."

A long silence made Jake anxious. He began drumming his fingers on his thighs. He was about to speak again when a loud cackle ripped the sheet-thin quiet.

The laugh turned into a choking cough sound. Rob's eyes became stern. "For what? Your mother put you up to this?"

Hands moving into his pockets, gazing at the floor, then up at his father, Jake stepped closer. "So you and mom don't get a divorce. There's something special that happens when people look into Tom's mirrors. They change. I've seen it, Dad."

Rob's cackling resumed. After catching his breath, he turned over so that his face was buried into the side of the couch. He spoke with a muffled voice. "I don't need to change a damn thing. Now go to bed."

Jake woke before dawn. He began grinding coffee beans. When he watched his dad roll out of his blanketed cocoon, he pulled his thumb off the noisy machine.

Rob got up off the sofa, rubbing his eyes. "Really? This early?"

Jake pushed out his chest and walked into the living room. "Dad, I want you to come and see Uncle Tom. Please."

Rob's eyes made a V shape. "What did I tell you? I'm not walking into that shop and looking into a god-damned mirror."

When Jake left for school, he noticed Jean's folder on the entrance table. There was a sticky note on it that read: *Rob. You have until the end of the week to sign. Don't let this get ugly.*

After school, Jake walked through Tom's tinted doors with a sluggish stride, his backpack dangling on his elbow.

"Bad day with the books?" Tom looked up from a pile of papers, smiling awkwardly. "I got to run a few errands. Look after the shop for thirty minutes. Then when I get back, you can get started on those windows again."

Jake nodded.

The shop's front door hadn't closed when the idea came to Jake to inspect the back room. He pressed his face against the tinted glass, peering past his reflection until he could make out Tom getting into his green Chevy.

Jake thought it over for a few minutes, then entered the mirror room through a purple door. Black acoustic foam panels covered the walls and roof. The floor was also black, a kind of linoleum tile. The corridor light slipping through gave just enough visibility for Jake to inspect the room. He saw a red velvet chair and a standing mirror in the corner. The same kind of mirror Rudy had purchased. Nervous to look into the mirror, Jake moved quickly behind it as he noticed a few of the acoustic panels had begun to lift off the wall. When he moved closer, he observed that the panels had been glued to a black door. Sweaty-palmed, Jake pushed down on the door handle and entered a space half the size of the mirror room. Jake pulled out his phone and pressed his flashlight button. There was a gap above the acoustic-paneled walls of the mirror room and the ceiling. Big spotlights were attached above the barrier, pointing into the mirror room.

A pile of mirrors stacked side by side stood in the corner of the backroom. Wires crisscrossed at Jake's feet, leaving little space for walking. He felt an anxiousness rise from his stomach and then settle in the back of his throat. He tried to swallow. As soon as he did, the lights above his head burst into a beautiful red, blue, yellow, orange, and green display. White-fisted, Jake tiptoed back to where he'd entered, towards the mirror room. When he peered around the edge of the black door, the spotlights above struck the mirror. The lights reflected into the mirror room a lovely magic-like kaleidoscope of colors. A sound like a howling wind came next. Jake followed the sound to the set of speakers hidden by the acoustic paneling. One ear leaning into the mirror room, the wind noise came from every direction.

"Testing. Testing. One, two, three." The wind sound stopped. Jake recognized Tom's voice. "Testing. One, two, three." Tom's voice was different a second time, boomier, like thunder. *Some kind of filter,* Jake thought.

"Look into the mirror and see." Tom continued. "Testing. Testing. Look into the mirror and see. And find. Yes. Find. Find for yourself that you have been searching in vain for something already within you."

Lights changing colors and shapes, Jake watched the mirror turn into what looked like water rushing from it, then a bright, burning sun that hurt his eyes, forcing him to look away.

"Do you see it?" The voice continued. Do you see all that is within you?"

Jake felt a strange pull towards the mirror. He ambled forward. Then he quickly backpedaled into hiding. Tom walked into the mirror room. Jake watched with steady eyes. Tom adjusted the angle of the mirror, then smiled and smacked his hands together. "All set for another fool."

The chimes crashed against the tinted shop window. "Be right there!" Tom hurried out. Jake followed with quiet steps.

"My son told me to come here. Said you have some kind of mirror that could help me. The name's Rob Snow." Rob's words struggled from his mouth. His torso swayed above his planted feet.

"Dad." Jake pushed in front of Tom. Rob pulled Jake into his sweaty chest. The tinted windows mirrored Jake's face. He could see Tom grinning behind him.

"Let's get out of here, Dad," Jake whispered.

Rob squared up face to face with his son. "She's going to leave me."

Gripping his dad's hands, Jake squeezed until he could feel Rob's bones. "She hasn't left you yet."

Jake slid his shop key on the counter. Then he looked at Tom dead in the eyes until the old man looked away.

"Find some other fool to clean your windows." The chimes banged against the tinted glass.

I Found a Love Hidden in a Backstreet

He was a giant of a man hunched in a rickety chair. The dark rings under his eyes looked as though colored in by a four-year-old with a purple marker. He puffed on the butt of his cigarette. His face went tight with every draw. A baseball cap covered what I presumed was a bald head, strands of wiry gray fraying out the sides.

"You looking for love, son?"

I pretended to watch the sea, my mind scattered in codes and international unrest.

He stood up. "I'm talking to you, son!"

I noticed his button-down shirt with screen-printed palm trees and his black chest hair sprouting out. He pushed his palms into a wooden table, a cup of coins between his hands. As I stepped closer, I noticed his tan loafers dotted with white paint.

He looked up and down my body. "You part of the cavalry?"

I couldn't go anywhere without stares, thank-you's, and kisses on the cheek from old ladies.

"I guess so."

Stopping on my belt buckle, he stepped closer. "Where's your gun?"

Removing my sunglasses and exaggerating my smile, I said, "I don't carry a gun."

He smiled with straight, bright teeth, hardly representative of life on the streets. "You're one of those funny nerd types, aren't you?"

Where there wasn't black on his fingers, the skin on his hands looked soft, more middle-aged than old, a disparity from the folds and wrinkles on his face.

As quickly as the grey smoke cloud from his mouth disappeared, I sniffed a foul mixture of sweat and carbon monoxide concocted as if in a lab, used for extracting information from captured enemies.

I feared I might taste it, so I kept my mouth wired shut.

"You deaf?"

A big wave smashed into the black rocks. I stepped back from the spray. "I know my way around a computer, you might say."

He stared up and down the street, then hunched forward. "You're not in charge of any nuclear codes, are you?"

I scrunched my nose, trying my best to keep the air out, then forced a smile. "Top secret. If I told you, I'd have to kill you."

The bell rang, and a young girl shouted, "Tommy! Order for Tommy."

I paid for my food and sat under a red oak tree. The man and I watched each other between cars and passers-by, hiding stares when our eyes crossed. As I took the last bite of my battered cod, he walked towards me.

The oak tree smelled pleasant. The man stood on the roots, his kneecaps blocking my view. His hairy legs looked like a network of black spiders crawling up and down, spinning webs.

"So, you must be looking for love, then?"

I swallowed the fish. I put a napkin over my nervous smile. "Why do you say that?"

He inched closer and pointed at my hand. "No ring, for starters, and you're a serviceman. That means you're not jaded. And you're young enough to be my son."

"She'll come one of these days. I ain't too worried."

He offered me his hand. "I know where she is."

If I weren't a man who came into contact with more screens than faces, I would've had the sense to laugh and wish him farewell.

"And where's that?" I said, half curious, half joking.

He pulled me to my feet. "I'll introduce you."

"I'm sorry, sir. Duty calls. Maybe tomorrow?"

I tried to yank my hand free, but his grip tightened. "Now, you'd be a real fool if you didn't follow me, son. I'm telling you."

"They only give me an hour," I said.

The soft purple under his eyes crinkled as his gaze narrowed. "You're scared of love, ain't you?"

By now, we'd drawn the attention of a few people walking their dogs.

I felt nervous with all the eyes on me. "I'll meet her, but just for a few minutes; then, I need to get back to work."

He dropped my hand. It fell to my side, white and slippery.

"Follow me, son."

The man walked faster than I'd seen him move from the table to the tree. Now his legs weren't stiff sticks. They looked strange underneath his old body, as though fitted artificially.

We stayed on the busy street until it meandered into narrow off-shoots and side alleys with run-down shops where you could get a car or TV repaired.

"C'mon, son. We're almost there."

He went left down a one-way wide enough for a bicycle. The buildings were derelict. Dark overhangs of busted corrugated iron pooled into shadows at our feet. I was about to turn around and escape without him noticing me when I saw her.

I rubbed my fingers on my eyelids, pulling the skin tight around my sockets.

She was a bright yellow rose in a coalfield.

Any other man might've questioned why she stood idly among broken glass and dented hubcaps.

"Patty, I've got somebody for you to meet."

I inched closer to my desert prophet, leaning on his words I'd suddenly come to believe.

She swayed. "Hello, soldier."

Her southern tone fell smoothly on my ears. I clambered in front of the man, hiding my nerves with a smile.

"Nice to meet you, P-P-P-Patty."

I kissed her hand. I felt a wild energy erupt in my stomach.

"You're a combat man?" She pulled her hand from my lips. Her eyes drifted towards the old man, then back to me.

"Not a combat man. A computer boy." The old man offered.

Her face softened.

"Well, I have basic combat training." I pushed my sunken chest into my shirt. "But yes, I work with computers mostly. I'm an expert of sorts."

Patty stepped closer. Her breath made the hair on my neck stand, and my palms began to sweat. "Tell me more about this computer work."

I stood conflicted, torn between the sworn allegiance to my government and her red lips. I had so much classified information I could share to bring her closer.

My training hadn't prepared me for this.

"Well, I'm in charge of the country's...."

Bam! Something struck the back of my head before a secret spilled. I drifted into darkness, searching for my bright yellow moon.

When I woke, pulsing pounds of pain ran from my neck to the top of my head, then back down again. My hand turned disco-red when I touched my cervical, wading upstream to the top of my skull.

I squirmed out of my shirt and pressed it against the gushing flow until small bones under my hand crunched in and out of place. I swore I'd kill him if he laid a finger on her. I reached for my phone in my pocket. My hand ran against my pants lining, finding only lint and scraps of paper. I checked the other pocket and then the back one. Everything was gone: phone, wallet, keys, passwords, security clearance cards. I tried to stand. Nothing felt right. My palms pressed against the concrete, lifting my weight, attempting to shift it to my soles. The black haze came at me like enemy fire, pushing me into a death bunker.

When I woke, the doctor called it a miracle and said I must have had a reason for coming back. The doctor was a tall, serious young man with pale-white skin. He ran through a checklist of questions with a blunt pencil. "Name. Date of birth. Occupation."

It hurt to recollect the information—even more to speak it.

"Some men are waiting outside to ask you further questions. Do you feel fine to speak with them?"

I peered behind his shoulders and saw five men in uniform; their faces leaned into the glass. One of the men was my boss, General James Bannon. The others I didn't know.

"Sure."

The men filed in; steps synced, eyes on each other's necks.

"Tim, I'm glad you're okay. They say you'll be fine."

I smiled.

"These men are part of the investigation committee: Sergeant Dean and Major Houk. Do you mind if they ask you a few questions?"

I nodded slowly.

"Mr. Wilkins, what do you remember leading up to the moment you received the blow to your head?"

Behind my eyes, her yellow dress appeared. I envisioned her dark, long legs, lean as marching lines.

"Mr. Wilkins?"

The back of my head burned with pain again.

The man questioning me, Sergeant Dean, had a solid and heavy voice much like his wide-shouldered frame.

I dragged my words. "He was an old man, smelled rotten like a mixture of smoke and sweat. He was wearing a hat, red, with a blue horse in the center of it. About as tall and big as you. Similar deep voice too, but with a different accent."

One of the men, wearing thick-rimmed glasses, scribbled on a notepad. The others listened, heads stiff, eyes pointed like sniper rifles.

"Was there anyone else with him?"

My pulse quickened.

"No, nobody whatsoever. He was all alone. Just him."

Their aim moved into each other's eyes with hands between whispers.

"Was there a woman, Tim?"

Dean's voice sounded like the cock of a shotgun.

I sat up, wires hanging from my arms. It hurt to look the big man in the eye. "I told you. It was an old man. He jumped me in an alley. Probably just wanted cash. That's all."

"Did you tell him anything?"

"About what?"

"Your job. The things you've been working on."

I breathed an agonizing mouthful of air. "Of course not! What kind of idiot do you think I am?"

The pitch of my voice surprised me. I withdrew and went down flat on my back again, afraid I'd overplayed it.

One of the men met my frustration with his own, veins protruding from his forehead. "He has everything. He didn't need to say a damn word to him."

I shot up, warring through jolting discomfort. "He was a tramp! He wouldn't know what to do with any of it."

Sergeant Dean stepped closer to me. "Now, now, Tim. Settle down. We're just trying to process this." General Bannon looked at the rest of them, sharp-eyed. "That'll be all for today, men. Let's give him time to rest."

*

Weeks later, I stood to my feet and left the hospital without the suggested cane or walker.

I returned to the place of the mugging, not expecting to find much. I packed my gun, though I figured that the old man was probably a ghost already.

The air smelled salty from the high breakers crashing against the rock wall, flinging wisps of foam into the main road. I crossed the street, retracing my steps to the tree, and stared at its roots, trying to recall the conversation that lured me away.

My recollections steered me from the shade into the back alleys, past buildings leaning into the street like waves about to break. A few men without shirts crowded around a cigarette and stared at me with dangerous eyes.

Continuing past the black abyss of burned cars, forgotten steel drum fires, and tires piled like pyramids, I searched for her. Then, stopping under a small neon sign above a staircase dangling from the roof by chords of rope, I read aloud.

"The Yellow Tulip"

I considered cupping my hands around my mouth and asking for help across the staircase. But going unnoticed around these parts seemed wiser. I tiptoed, gripping the frayed rope, thick red and blue veins striping my arms. Before I took my final step at the top, I raised my chest and inhaled a filthy blend of smoke and perfume. A small hand fell into mine. I squeezed it.

"How may I help you, sir?" Her dress was near-identical, a little shorter above the middle of her thighs, but it displayed the same soft stretch cotton, flared cut, and wide round neck. She wore a black belt that added sophistication. In my lightheaded agitation, I thought it was Patty. I squeezed her soft hand a little harder. She pulled away. The sadness of it alerted me to this woman's pale face and leathery skin.

"I'm looking for a girl in a yellow dress."

She smiled. Then, I heard a chuckle she tried to hide as she stepped out of the way. She extended her hand to a room filled with men sipping beers and yellow-dressed women with trays in their hands.

I moved forward against my better judgment, tilting my head to the lady at the entrance. I bought a drink. My neck hurt. Every stolen look resulted in a pretty face approaching me with the offer of time in a back room or a motel down the road. My description of her could've fit all ten of them. "I'm okay. Thank you." I kept saying.

As the afternoon turned into evening, the tables and seats around the bar grew packed with men from work with ties undone and jackets left in the car. I watched hollow, straight faces turn bright red and fill with a kind of energy that only ignites with unbridled passion. This unholy fascination with men growing drunker, desire spilling out on all sides, momentarily overtook my search for her.

I snapped out of my daze as a man walked through the door, looking oddly familiar. He wore a loose-fitting shirt that couldn't hide his massive shoulders. He hid his face under a red cap with a symbol in the center. Curious, I left my chair and half-empty glass. I nudged closer to the man, hiding behind a fake plant.

"Where's Patty?"

It couldn't be, I thought—that booming voice demanding my immediate attention, the beggar, Sergeant Dean. I bent my neck around the green plastic leaf. My skin stretched. My scabs cracked. I felt warm blood begin to stream. I jumped back in panic, knocking the plant to the ground. Sergeant Dean turned around. My body went shaky seeing the blue horse on his red hat.

"Good evening, soldier."

I struggled to my feet, a hand on my hip. "You bastard. It was you!"

He walked with slow, deliberate, thudding steps, a smile widening across his lips. "I have no idea what you're talking about."

Small red spots stained my shoes. The pain from my neck disappeared into a boiling bath of rage, filling my veins. I removed my gun and stretched out my arms. I curled my finger lightly on the trigger. "Tell me every-thing, or I'll kill you."

A collective gasp filled the air. The pretty women in yellow dresses screamed with fear. The only exit be-came a narrow tunnel.

My enemy stopped an arm's length from the barrel of my gun. His grin and calm demeanor provoked my anger further.

"You're not shooting anybody tonight. Nobody'll be-lieve you, Tim. Nobody."

My hands rattled. I pushed the pistol into his palms. "Why'd you do it?"

He wrapped his fingers over the silver barrel. I could've blown his entire hand off.

"Why does anybody betray his country?"

Patty walked in from a back room. Her dark, irre-sistible legs were three-quarters on display. My mouth opened involuntarily. I moved my eyes across her, ac-celerating the pulse beating furiously within me.

Her sea-blue eyes fell into mine. "Tim, you're okay."

I couldn't believe she remembered my name. My grip on the trigger softened. My stiff, outstretched arms went spaghetti-like. The pistol dropped to my side.

"Yes, they say I'm going to be…"

I was all vision in sunlight. Sergeant Dean charged towards my knees with his big, round shoulders. I pulled the gun up from my thigh and pointed it at the horse on his head. The collision was swift. I fired two shots before falling to the ground in a blur. When I opened my eyes, both of them lay outstretched on the floor. Blood and brain matter were spattered on the walls like vomit. I crawled past Sergeant Dean and pressed my ear into Patty's chest. But the only sound I could hear was the song playing on the jukebox. *I found a love, hidden in a backstreet.*

Smoked Salmon for Lunch

I was biting into a smoked salmon sandwich when Pretty walked up to me. I would've been too afraid to look at her if she hadn't spoken.

"That's a nice tie," she said as she furled it in her fingers, then pulled it tight. Choking on my sandwich, I tried to spit it out. It landed a big gooey mess on my black, shiny penny loafers.

She let go of my tie and patted me on the back, giggling. "Oh, I'm sorry, honey. I didn't mean to scare you."

I examined her face and started choking again. Her skin was soft and rich, and a beautiful olive tint that made her blue eyes look like rare opals in a museum.

She touched my arm. An electrical shock buzzed through my body.

I wiped my sleeve over my mouth, cleaning the little bit of dribble from my cowboy mustache.

"Howdy," I said, making my voice sound solid and deep.

She shook my hand. "My name's Pretty. I think I've seen you here before."

Her palm was delicate. I held it until she pulled away.

"I come here for lunch almost every day." I said.

I tried to keep eye contact, but looking at her felt uncomfortable and exhilarating.

"And where does such an important-looking man like you work?" Her accent was southern, but I couldn't tell from which state exactly. Though I'd studied and perfected the Texas Drawl for a former undercover assignment, I was from Minnesota, naturally pronouncing O's and A's longer than the I-90.

Pointing to the grassy hill behind Sam's Fish Shop, I cleared my throat, "Somewhere in that direction."

Pretty followed my finger with meticulous movements from her head.

"I normally carry a pair of binoculars, but you've caught me empty-handed today." I laughed nervously, hoping she'd find my joke funny.

Instead, she kept staring at the hill with a serious expression. I felt more comfortable gazing at her with her eyes turned from mine, and I hoped I could keep watching her until my lunch break was over.

"What does such a handsome man like you do for a living?"

My heart accelerated as she turned around to look at me. Though my facial expression felt strained and uncomfortable, I pushed my chest out and straightened my neck.

I had five job narratives prepared and memorized. Judging by Pretty's red lipstick, tight pink dress, and zebra-skinned handbag slung over her shoulder, I thought the Wall Street trader persona would impress her most. Glancing at my watch, I realized I only had ten minutes before my break was up.

"I'm a stock trader." Standing, I twirled my mustache in my fingers.

"I'm afraid I do need to get going, though. Shall we meet again?" My confidence surprised me.

Pretty's face softened with a beautiful smile and glow. She grabbed my hand and squeezed. "That would be wonderful. But I don't even know your name."

I'm not sure I'd ever felt my heart beating so fast. Stammering, I replied, "Melvin." I hadn't shared my real name with anybody in years. I tried to recover. "But most people call me Pete."

Her eyebrows furrowed into a neat V shape.

I laughed nervously. "It's a long story."

"I like Melvin," she said, smiling, squeezing, and rubbing my bony knuckles in her fingertips. "Lunch tomorrow? Same time? Same place?"

"Wonderful. What do you like to eat? My treat."

"Oh, you don't have to do that, Melvin. I know how to feed myself."

"No. No. I insist." I pushed my knuckles into her palm, and she squeezed tighter.

"Well, only if you let me buy the next day?"

I hadn't had much luck or experience with women, so I wasn't sure whether to take her offer or keep insisting I buy. Then, the thought of kissing her flashed through my mind, and I almost acted on it.

My radio beeped. Pretty's hand fell to her side as I let it go. I hugged her awkwardly, "Sounds good, Pretty. I'll see you tomorrow."

I saw a sticky note attached to my computer when I entered my office. "Come see me immediately." I read it in a low whisper, then turned to see Colonel Higgs glaring at me from behind his glass window.

"You're five minutes late, soldier."

I pressed my hands against my thighs and stood unsteady. "Sorry, Sir. Won't happen again."

"Where were you? You realize the importance of this mission, don't you, Melvin?" Higgs' eyes looked like sharp sticks.

Making eye contact with him while I spoke was challenging, so I centered my vision on a small mole just above his left eyebrow. "The line at Sam's was rather long today. I'm very sorry, Sir. I assure you, this mission is my highest priority. You have my word."

As I sat down at my desk and resumed my algorithmic coding, the prevention of World War Three didn't seem quite as crucial. Instead of studying the numbers and letters running across my screen, I replayed the earlier moments with Pretty. The data on my monitor was a haze. As I strained my eyes to study it, the rapid transmission of information contorted into the shape of Pretty's face. With a slow raising of my head, I peered over my workstation and was relieved to see Higgs in a tunnel of work. I opened a private search window. I typed *Girls named Pretty in Dripping Springs, Texas.*

"Melvin! Get in here immediately!"

My index finger drummed on the mouse, closing the window on an inappropriate image.

"Who in God's name is this?" On Colonel Higgs' computer screen was a picture of Pretty holding my hand. Thankfully, her face was unrecognizable, turned away from the camera.

"Where did you get this?" I stammered.

Slapping his hands on his desk, he knocked the mouse onto the floor, splitting the plastic casing into two.

I stepped back, afraid of where his rage might take him.

"You trying to catch a ride down the Mystic River? Don't lie to me, now, soldier."

"She's an old cousin of mine. Haven't seen her in a while." I made sure to speak quickly, giving him little opportunity to detect any faltering in my voice. That's how they'd trained us. Speak fast and with eyes locked on a single target.

"Cousins!?" Colonel Higgs blasted his index finger onto the screen.

I refocused my eyes on the mole above his eyebrow. "She's always been very affectionate, Sir. Such a wild coincidence to see her at Sam's today. I haven't seen her since she returned from Vietnam."

"Vietnam?"

"Teaching English as a Second Language."

"There's still a lot of commies in that country. You know that, right?"

"Don't worry, Sir. She's a patriot."

"Cousin or hooker, you compromise this mission, and I'll chain you up myself. You hear me?" Higgs clicked on a blue file icon in the corner of his screen. "You see the latest? Know what it means yet?"

I removed my glasses, squinting, moving closer to his screen. It was the same data I'd gotten lost in moments earlier. "Not yet, Sir. But give me a few minutes, and I'll decipher it."

I couldn't sleep that night, thinking about Pretty and how Colonel Higg's had acquired that photo of us holding hands. I would've noticed a drone flying, even the low-noise ones emitting less than 71DBs. Somebody must have been watching us. She didn't deserve that kind of disrespect. Neither did I.

Ten minutes before my lunch break the following day, I lied to Higgs, "I need to adjust our wireless connection, Sir. Communications are lagging every so slightly. I'll have a look, then head to lunch."

I didn't like carrying a gun. I kept it in my satchel. I felt the barrel tip digging into my spine as I jogged the path to Sam's. When I stopped to catch my breath, I felt compelled to remove my gun underneath the shade of a giant oak tree, first looking around to see if anybody was following me. Satisfied, I shoved the gun into my front pocket. When I reached Sam's, only a few people were waiting in line.

I almost tripped, losing the salmon sandwiches, when I saw the back of Pretty's head, walking towards her. She sat on a faded red bench, watching birds fight over seed. Setting the food gently to the ground, I repositioned the gun and made a final round with my eyes.

"I hope you're hungry!" I shouted in my deepest voice, startling her as she jumped up.

"You frightened me, Melvin! How wonderful it is to see you again!" Pretty tugged on her short, tight blue skirt, making it challenging to keep my eyes from her luscious thighs.

"What did you get for lunch?" Her question redirected my gaze. When I lifted my eyes, I knew she'd seen me staring at her legs.

"Smoked salmon sandwiches. Is there anything else?" I managed.

"My favorite! Come and sit next to me, Melvin."

My arms began shaking, and my feet felt like lead as I slowly approached her. She was even more beautiful than the previous day.

When I sat down, she grabbed my hand and stroked her fingers back and forth over my knuckles. "I'm so glad to spend a little time with you today."

I wanted to look at her but felt that I wouldn't be able to talk if I did. "Me too," I said, staring at my polished penny loafers.

"Any big trades today, Melvin?" She nibbled on her sandwich like caviar, slow, small bites.

Buying time, I shoved the food into my mouth, holding up my hand. Pretty looked away. As I followed her eyes, I noticed two men wearing in-ear radios walking toward us with their hands in their coat pockets. I focused on my shadow, hoping they wouldn't detect that I'd noticed them. The way the sun angled onto my body made my shoulders appear as round boulders. I slipped a hand into my pocket, gripping the gun, feeling the trigger on my index finger.

"It's her! Now. Move-in! Move-in!"

"Melvin!" Pretty's sandwich fell out of her hand as she hurled her arms around me.

The men pointing their guns at us were part of the security detail from my office building. "Mr. Blakeman, this woman isn't who you think she is."

Pretty's grip tightened. Her tears soiled my chest.

"I don't understand," I said, pulling the gun from my pocket. Pretty must have felt the tip of the barrel against her because no sooner had I removed the gun had she snatched it from me. She fired it in less than a second, killing both men with two perfect shots between their eyes.

Before I could say a word, Pretty pushed the gun into my temple. "I hate Salmon almost as much as I hate democracy."

The Path to Owl River

I kissed Suzy on the forehead, wondering how many more chances I'd get to do so.

"Be careful, Sam." she said. "That leopard's still out there, you know? I've seen photos online of it."

"I will."

"Make sure Fred brings his gun!"

It brought an unusual feeling driving past Fred's house without picking him up. I was surprised to feel a new courage occupy the always-with-me nervous, anxious place in my chest. I drove slowly, watching Fred throw his kids in the air in his beautiful, manicured yard. A part of me hoped he'd seen me, fishing rod strapped to the roof of my Prius, moving towards the sunset.

I kept my eyes in the mirror until Fred's house disappeared. When I parked my Prius at the Owl River trailhead, I stopped to look at the set of descending stairs leading toward the ocean. I set my rod on my tackle box and backpack, then began a gentle jog down the stairs towards the sea. In ten years of fishing Owl River with Fred, I'd never seen the beach below the stairs.

The moon cast a luminous glow onto the water, making the slow-moving current seem alive.

I gazed until it felt like the ripply surface was peering into my soul. I returned up the stairs, grabbed my fishing gear, and began on the path toward Owl River.

Entering the tunnel forest of darkness, my attention fixed on the screams of monkeys, birds chirping, and the likelihood of snakes and scorpions at my feet. With one hand, I clutched my flashlight, with the other my rod. Only ten feet in, I began stopping every few minutes to ensure there weren't wild animals stalking me, slowly turning my neck and moving my eyes quickly in a circle. Before stepping forward after the final pause, Doctor Simpson's words flashed across my mind.

Earlier that day, I'd gone in for my yearly check-up.

"Well, I don't know how to say this, Mr Silk." Dr. Simpson kneeled in front of me.

"You have maybe a month to live, more if you take it easy and arrange for hospice."

"What!?" I paused, waiting for him to tell me he'd made a mistake.

His eyes were still and cold.

"I'm only thirty-eight! I feel great. What are you talking about!?"

"I'm sorry, Mr. Silk. But, unfortunately, sometimes symptoms don't even manifest until…Well…You know."

With Dr. Simpson's words rattling in my mind, I traversed the first quarter of the trail, the blackest, steepest part.

The path flattened out, following the spine of Ash Mountain. Usually, before continuing, Fred would lay out his palm and wait for me to hand him his carton of cigarettes and lighter. My tackle box had a special compartment where Fred preferred to store his stash. "In case of rain," he'd say with a grave expression, handing me a new carton. I'd sit and wait for Fred on a small bench while he insisted on taking a minor yet dangerous detour to observe the bay from the perched overlook. He'd light his cigarette and dangle his feet off the cliff face. "C'mon, Sam! Come have a smoke with me!"

"Cancer, Fred! You ever heard of it?"

"Fine! Then just come look at this view! It's incredible!"

It was the only occasion I was grateful for Fred's smoking addiction, any excuse to avoid my fear of heights. "Secondhand smoke!" I'd shout, "You ever heard of it!?"

As I set my tackle box and rod on the bench, I wished I'd taken Fred up on one of his thousand offers: just one smoke I coughed my way through with burning eyes.

I opened the compartment, grabbed Fred's cigarettes and lighter, then began with stiff legs towards the overlook. The moon spotlighted my steps from under the canopy of thick fern trees. The fear I felt from the narrow trail and looking down the steep walls of the cliff face stopped me for a second, almost causing me to turn around. Then, for some odd reason, I thought of Suzy's upcoming thirtieth birthday and the Alaskan cruise I'd decided against because of budget constraints. I'd book it if I returned home and make sure the tickets were transferrable, I thought. A big flat rock shone underneath the night sky. I could almost see Fred hanging his feet off the edge, watching him blow rings of smoke toward the horizon.

Resting on the rock, I now understood the conviction and insistence of Fred's pleading. It felt like praying, scanning the valley below, discovering what my eyes could find from such a vantage point. I watched the town's lights flicker and fade until only the moon's silver shine lingered on. I lit a cigarette. I coughed, then barked as the poisonous graze of carbon monoxide coated my throat and lungs. Before long, it felt like I was floating somewhere near the horizon. I thought about lighting another when the ride evened out, but the dark path to Owl River lay waiting.

The final patch of fern-clouded forest descended toward the river's mouth. I turned off my flashlight and stood in the darkness, motionless and aware of all the sounds of wild animals and the dirty river throwing herself into the arms of the sea.

I heard twigs breaking slowly, rhythmically, getting louder with every snap. The leopard, I thought. I wanted at least one chance at catching a fish before being eaten alive. I grabbed a few pebbles at my feet and threw them toward where I'd heard the twigs snapping. I sprinted the final downhill to Owl River, skidding across the worn-out earth, dust on my lips, shouting, "Don't look back, Sam! Don't you dare look back!"

Out of breath, I flung my rod, tackle box, and backpack onto the rocks as I emerged from the forest. I jumped into the river, hoping the leopard couldn't swim. I watched the clearing for a minute, only the top of my head above the shimmering brown surface of the water. I thought I saw the trees rustle. I rubbed my eyes, then opened them again to see a canopy of motionless leaves and limbs. I waded to the rocks, tasting the salt on my tongue. I pulled myself out of the river, then fitted my rod with tackle and bait. I was accustomed to Fred tying everything for me except the swivel. He'd have his line in the water by the time I'd pick up my sinker from the tackle box. "Give me that, Sam, before you hurt somebody with it." I'd watch him work his little fingers like Suzy's needles through her winter sweaters.

I dropped my line into a deep gulley. I'd only cast beyond the gulley two or three times before, and on every attempt, my hook got stuck on a barnacle or rock. Fred would watch my line drop into the gulley and look up at me with the same endearing face as when he'd offered me a cigarette. "One of these days, you'll have to venture out of your kiddie pool, Sam."

But Fred never looked, just chuckled to himself, landing his bait safely in the chaos of the churning tide.

To hell with it, I thought. If only Fred could see me now.

I cast beyond the gulley into the crashing waves. Instantly, the ocean dragged me forward so fiercely that I had to cement my heels into the black rock to avoid falling into the water.

My quads strained as I fought the sea's incredible power. I noticed my rod's tip bending like cardboard.

"A fish," I shouted in the silver-lit darkness. "I've got a real fish over here!"

Spinning my reel, feeling as though my blood-pumped wrist was going to explode, I heard Fred as if he was standing next to me. *Don't fight it. Let the fish tire out, then spin that reel like a merry-go-round when it's got nothing left.*

I followed Fred's advice, and after an eternity, I reeled in the biggest fish I'd ever caught. The only fish I'd ever caught.

I was too excited to offer myself or the fish to the leopard.

I ran back to the parking lot without stopping for breath or a cigarette. Both hands clutching to the bottom of my backpack, I made sure the bloody fish wasn't flopping up and down, spraying its guts. I walked into the parking lot, breathing heavily. As I tied my rod to the roof of my car, Suzy's Subaru came screeching in, driver and passenger doors flinging open. "Sam! Thank God! You're okay!" Suzy screamed, sprinting towards me. "When Fred called, I knew you'd gone alone. I was afraid something awful happened to you!"

"Saw you drive past my house, Sam-O. With your rod on your roof." Fred got out of the passenger side, wearing his big smile, walking toward me. "Called your lady and asked if you'd met Jesus."

I wiped my fish-blood-covered hands down my pants, opened my backpack, and pulled out my fish. "Look what I caught. Isn't she beautiful?"

Fred hurried closer while Suzy backed away.

"What a beauty! How'd you snag that bugger!? Bigger than any fish I ever caught!"

"I guess I learned something all these years with you." I lifted the fish into Fred's cradled arms and grinned as his knees and back bent to hold its weight.

"Dr. Simpson called moments after you left the house, Sam." Suzy stepped closer.

I'd forgotten about Dr. Simpson. Hearing his name made my body droop. "So you know?" I said.

"Know what?"

My eyes felt sunken as I stared at Suzy. "What did he say?"

"To find you immediately. To tell you that he'd made a terrible mistake on your report. That you're as healthy as a May morning."

Fred was still admiring my fish. I kneeled to open my tackle box, grabbed three cigarettes, lit them, and puff-coughed until the orange glow appeared. I handed one to Suzy and Fred, wrapped my arms around their necks, pulling them tight onto the tops of my shoulders.

The smoke made the moon look hazy. I kissed Fred on the cheek, then Suzy on the lips, smiling. "She's a beauty, isn't she?"

The Bridge Across Inkar Ravine

Marlon spent the pre-dawn hours praying on his knees. He kissed his wife, Rebecca, and their only child, James, before saddling Stalworth, then fitting himself with armor. When the council formed a year prior, only Marlon and a few of his friends held the opinion that building a bridge across Inkar Ravine would inflict more harm than good.

They whispered to each other in the tavern at night. "In the dark, I've seen all kinds of fire shooting into that yonder sky. Why do we want anything to do with that?"

"And the screams! Loud as a weeping child!"

"Those glass eyes think there's something in it for us. They say there's trees that touch the clouds. Green as moss. And the way winter ripped us apart. They think our future's going to be 'cross the boards of that bridge!"

The village craftsmen commissioned to the bridge earned double their wage working night and day, seven days a week, pounding steel-tipped hammers with calloused hands. Young boys, too small to touch their soles to the stirrups, gathered bits of bread and filled buckets with water for their fathers. They watched sweat pour down their daddy's brows, measuring the progress of toil by throwing stones off the bridge's expanding edge.

Once the bridge neared its halfway point, the council called a mandatory meeting for all healthy men and women between the ages of eighteen and thirty-five.

Rebecca hid a suckling James under her shirt as Marlon led her by the hand into the tavern. Standing room only, Marlon barged in between a group of young men and secured a spot against the back wall.

"We need to get a little closer," Rebecca urged. "We're not going to be able to hear anything, darling."

"What's to hear?" Marlon replied, his eyes drifting between the tops of the heads of his fellow citizens.

"Please, Marlon! Don't be like this. Not now."

James peeked out of Rebecca's shirt, whispering, "Mama. Mama."

Marlon cupped his big, leathered palm on his son's head, then nudged the men before him. When the men recognized Marlon, they made room, and Marlon and Rebecca moved forward.

"Townspeople, thank you for your attendance on this momentous occasion!" Town mayor Hamilton Levy had a shaky voice whenever he spoke to a large group of people, and he flailed his arms about him like a puppet on a string.

"Like we had a choice," Marlon mumbled, eyes glaring straight into the tip of Levy's sharp dagger nose.

Levy continued. "As you know, the day of completion for our beloved bridge is fast approaching. We've deliberated long and hard about our best option for contacting the people beyond Inkar Ravine. I'm pleased to announce that one of you, one special individual in this room, will receive the honor of representing our people, touching hands with the foreigner, and paving a course for our tomorrow!"

A collective gasp echoed in the room. Then, before the whispers became too loud, Levy waved his hands and shouted, "Now. Now. Settle down! The best is yet to come."

Rebecca pushed forward, tugging Marlon's hand. Marlon cemented his feet. Rebecca gave him a cold stare and mouthed something he couldn't understand. Marlon cleared through several more groups of people until he, Rebecca, and James were standing right underneath the hook of Mayor Levy's nose.

"The perfect candidate will possess both intellectual and physical aptitude—a warrior who can wield his words as powerfully as his sword. We're offering a handsome reward for the winning candidate. A bounty that will ensure prosperity for generations to come."

Gasping gave way to murmuring, then loud cheering and foot stomping.

"Here. Here!" Levy yelled. "Ladies and gentlemen, may I please have your attention!"

The jeering, clapping, and jumping continued.

"Silence!" Levy screamed. "Silence! All of you!"

But the crowd continued in wild elation.

Then, above the noise, Marlon's baritone voice boomed.

"And what guarantees do we get that they don't chop off our heads for invading their territory?"

The room went silent. All eyes fixed on Marlon.

"Don't be ridiculous," Levy said with a nervous break in his voice. "These people are not barbarians. We've seen their bright night skies and trees that touch God's feet. How do you suppose such beauty can mingle with such horror?"

"Then why don't you go!" Marlon sneered.

Sensing the anger in Marlon's voice, Rebecca grabbed his hand, whispering, "Enough."

Marlon's strong shoulders wilted under his thick neck, and he became silent.

Levy straightened, making himself appear taller. "We'll begin our selection process at dawn on the banks of Tebb's River."

That night, once Rebecca had laid James down to sleep, she approached Marlon. "Will you go? For me. For us?"

Marlon didn't reply until she set her soft lily-white hand on his broad forearm. "And what if I don't come back?"

"Why are you so worried about the people on the other side? Nothing is going to happen to you. This is your time, Marlon. If not for yourself, then for James and me."

Marlon drummed his knuckles on the pine table he'd made for Rebecca during the previous year's winter. "And the bounty? If there weren't a bounty, would you feel the same? So convinced about the lines drawn for me in the twilight? I've seen how you look at those women dressed in silk. How you stare at their jeweled fingers."

The veins on Rebecca's throat began to protrude. "There's nothing wrong with wishing for more, Marlon. For wanting a better way of life for our son. Our son's sons. You've wasted your gifts. For what? So you don't have to face the fear of being something more. Here's your chance! Our chance!"

Marlon kept his eyes so perfectly still on the moon that his vision became hazy white. His fists tensed. He began digging his knuckles into the wood. With folded arms, Rebecca stood, watching him, her mouth wide open, her bottom lip quivering every so often.

Marlon extended his hands through the table, clicking his elbows as they locked, holding his weight to stand him up. He turned to Rebecca and pulled her into his wide-barreled chest. "I'll go if it's what you want. I'll go for you and James."

*

The crescent moon gave little light for Marlon's path to the bridge. Village people accompanied him with torches, cheering in hushed tones. Mayor Levy placed a wreath of Marigolds around Marlon's neck and shook his hand, saying, "May peace accompany your journey. Courage and favor, Marlon Jennings!"

The wooden beams creaked beneath Stalworth's hooves. Marlon looked over the side of his saddle. He almost tumbled as the ravine's bottomless pit glared up at him with its hungry rock-faced teeth. He heard the crowd gasp as Stalworth veered, bumping his head against the railing. Marlon straightened his beast, thumping Stalworth's ribs with his foot, sending the horse thundering across the bridge. Approaching the end of the bridge, Stalworth slowed to a gentle trot.

"Easy, boy."

Touching his feet to the ground, Marlon bent and felt the soil, pinching the black earth, smelling it between his fingertips. He noted how the trees in front of him looked just like the ones in his village.

Leading Stalworth, the other hand on the hilt of his sword, Marlon walked with slow, methodical steps towards the trail of smoke slithering upwards. He froze and knelt when he heard the song of a morning bird overhead. Marlon removed his wreath of marigolds. He hid them in a shrub, then rose and continued towards the smoke.

The path was well-worn and wide and dented with hoof prints. Marlon focused on listening for the laughs and cries of children and the blows of hammers against steel and timber. He heard nothing. Then, just as the scent of the smoke began to irritate his nostrils, a team of riders appeared from behind a cluster of trees.

"Stop where you are!" cried the middle horseman.

Marlon lowered his sword with a steady hand and began patting Stalworth. "I mean no harm," Marlon said.

"Why are you here? Did you come alone? Across that bridge you built?"

Marlon straightened, standing tall. "It's only me. And I have little reason to be here except that my village believes our communities may benefit from each other."

The middle rider jumped off his horse. "Say more, pilgrim."

Marlon stepped closer, looking back to his village every so often as he spoke. "We have strong men, and beautiful women. Our children listen to their elders. While we don't have a surplus of food, we always have enough to eat, and enough water to drink." Marlon moved his hand across the silky skin of one of the men's horses.

The leader turned to look at his men with a smile. "Sounds like your village is a wonderful place."

The horseman nodded and smiled.

Marlon raised his eyes to study the trees. "We've seen your lights at night, and while these pines don't appear as wonderfully green now, they glow gloriously from the other side of Inkar Ravine."

"What lights?" The leader snarled.

"Bright fire in the sky booming like thunder," Marlon replied.

The harsh lines on the leader's face softened. His shoulders appeared to grow heavy. "I only wish it was as you think it is."

"What do you mean?" Marlon asked.

"Those lights you see are the attacks of the northern invaders." Looking towards the north, the soldier pointed to a ridge above the tree line.

"Great explosions of fire dropping like stones, burning us alive. If we don't find a way to stop them, they'll come for your people next."

The soldier on the left jumped off of his horse. "Giant explosions of fire falling from the sky," he said again.

Marlon stared up as if expecting to see something. He slowly approached the men, narrowing his eyes on them. "I know what I must do."

All three of the soldiers were on their feet now. "What?" the leader muttered.

Marlon turned towards the bridge, walking towards Stalworth. Hitting his horse on the hind, Marlon jumped on his beast and screamed, "Run, boy! Run!" Stalworth was halfway across the bridge before the soldiers could mount their saddles. Marlon drew his sword and cut the ropes of the bridge. From the other side of Inkar Ravine, the soldiers watched the bridge crash into the rocks below.

The crowd was still there when Marlon made it back across.

"What did you discover?" Mayor Levy shouted above the cheers.

"Savages!" Marlon replied. "Out for the blood of our children!"

Marlon found Rebecca and James, lifted them onto his saddle, then slapped Stalworth until the beast's trot turned into a gallop.

Billy and the Priest

Father Sampson found me passed out on the curb outside his church. He let me use his shower and gave me a clean set of clothes and a half-eaten peanut butter sandwich. When he drove me to Ma's house that night, he asked her if I could have my old room back. He said I'd go to mass and promised that he'd get me on the straight and narrow.

"How many times we been through this now, Billy? Tell the priest, damn it!" Ma shouted as the three of us stood on her porch, my bloodshot eyes staring at my dirty feet.

"I'll get him right, Mrs. Clover. Please find it in your heart to give him another chance. There's no shortage of second chances in God's kingdom."

The first five clean days were always the toughest. I was watching TV, sitting on Ma's big brown leather sofa, when the tips of my fingers started to burn, then spread through the rest of my body. I jumped up and rubbed myself against the wall like a love-starved cat.

Ma was sipping cold coffee at the kitchen table. "You itching for it, ain't ya, Billy?"

"First few days are tough. But I'm trying, Ma."

"I smell even a trace of it, and you're out. Ya, hear me?"

I nodded, not looking at her, afraid of her cold eyes.

Ma had a nose like a bloodhound. A week without meth was the longest I'd ever gone since getting hooked on the stuff. I'd never really made a concentrated effort to give it up, and this occasion, I'd decided, was no different. The Sunday after my first mass was when I got the idea.

Father Sampson invited me into the vestry after the benediction. He told me to wait in line behind some folks who looked a bit new to church, like me. I studied a giant skull tattoo on the scalp of the bald man in front of me, then soon got distracted by a woman pacing in a small circle, whispering, "Jesus of Nazareth, Son of God, Jesus of Nazareth, Son of God."

After Father Sampson met with the man and then the woman, he called for me to come in.

The vestry was tiny. The walls were an awful cream color, resembling unpasteurized milk. Only a small glimmer of light spilled through one little, shoulder-height window. I stood in a corner next to the giant bronze cross the altar boy had carried during the service.

"Not as holy in here as we make it out to be, is it, Billy? Now let me count the collection, and then we'll get going for lunch." Father Sampson removed his liturgical vestments and undid a bun that was holding a swath of thick, curly brown hair.

"So that's why you're called Father Sampson," I said.

He laughed, "I guess so."

"Where's Delilah?"

"A student of the Old Testament. Impressive, my boy!"

The offering plate was a silver giant ashtray, filled with cash upwards of a thousand dollars. I watched him count the money and retrieve a key beneath the purple flower planter on the window sill.

"There's a 'P' in my name. I like to think of that 'P' as representing the promise of God's grace, keeping me from all vice."

"What's that?" I said, bypassing his reply, intrigued by a glass box I noticed in the cabinet.

"Vice?"

"No. That." I pointed.

"This?" He held up the box.

"Yeah."

"Not many people know about this. But, just between us, it's worth a whole lot of money. Enough to build five more churches like this one, I reckon."

"What is it?" I asked, walking towards the cabinet, eyebrows raised, studying the cork inside the glass container.

"It's from the bottle of wine that was used for communion when the pope visited a few years ago. I saved it."

"They let you do that?"

The glass box rested in his palm, a glint in his eyes. "Why not? I mean, I didn't really feel the need to ask anyone, you know? I just thought it would be nice to save, to memorialize such a special occasion."

Father Sampson handed the artifact to me as though it were a baby bird that had just been born. "Here, have a look. It still has a little wine stain on it. You see that?"

I made sure not to study the cork for long, setting the glass container back into the cabinet, then pretending to be distracted by the purple flower on the window sill.

"It's a violet," he said.

"What?"

"The plant you seem so interested in."

Furling the small leaves in his fingertips, Father Sampson smiled, gazing at the flower as though it were animate. "I suppose a struggling violet is more like it."

"Oh yes, yes," I managed, turning my gaze from the base of the plant, under which he'd set the key to the cabinet. "My mother has one just like it."

He sprayed water on the browning leaves. "Is that right?" he said, craning his neck to make eye contact. He set the water bottle down and approached with narrowing eyes and lips pressing into each other like one faint pencil-traced line. "How are things going at home, Billy?"

The grandfather clock chimed. The loud gong made me step back, bumping my head against the wall. "I guess that means it's time for lunch, Father!"

Father Sampson grinned, halting. "Well, I suppose it is, son. Where would you like to eat today? Promise me you won't tell anybody about that cork. Our secret, okay?"

I watched him put his keys in his coat pocket, the same set of keys he'd later set underneath the lemon tree outside.

"Your secret's safe with me, Father, but only because you're buying me lunch," I said, smiling.

When we reached his car, a blonde-headed lady, wearing a short red miniskirt, was waiting for him, leaning up against the car hood. As soon as Father Sampson noticed her, he hurried forward, whispered in her ear, and then she was gone.

"Your Delilah?" I asked, adjusting the seatbelt.

He smiled a kind of forced smile, then he laughed awkwardly. "Oh no, Billy. That was just a parishioner needing prayer."

*

As I parked Ma's old Toyota, stray cats scrambled into hiding. I watched and waited, gloved hands on the steering wheel.

I pulled my mask down, readjusting it. "You got this, Billy. You damn well got this." I took a deep breath through my nose, then slowly opened the car door.

Approaching the backside of the church, I stopped near the small lemon tree. The motion light flashed. I almost fell back down the steep brick stairs. I ducked below a freshly cut hedge and surveyed my surroundings. Crawling to the lemon tree, I carefully watched the busy street and the nearby houses. I lifted the potted tree with the tips of my fingers, then swiftly grabbed the keys with my other hand.

The second key I tried opened the backdoor to the church. Before locking the bolt behind me, I gazed at the cats for a minute or two. When an ambulance whizzed by with its dizzying red-white lights, I slammed the church door and tiptoed toward the altar. Two gold-laced candles burned on the altar table. I grabbed one and walked towards the vestry, careful not to spill any wax on the blood-red carpet. The same key I'd used to open the church door fit the vestry door. A light turned on from a house across the street, shining like a giant sun through the small vestry window. I shuddered and spilled wax onto the grandfather clock. Setting the candle next to the clock, I switched on the floor lamp and then drew the curtains shut. The violet looked even less alive in the low light, shriveled brown-grey leaves drooping below faded purple petals. A leaf flaked off the stem and feathered to the floor as I lifted the pot and found the cabinet key. When I removed the glass container from the cabinet, I noticed the collection plate full of cash. I stuffed a few hundred dollar bills into my pocket and pulled off my ski mask. I studied the cork wide-eyed. The latch on the casing didn't move as I tugged on it, stuck as though glued to the hinge. I shook the container with measured force, scared the cork might get scuffed. A stone crucifix lay on a pile of papers on the cabinet shelf. I grabbed it and slammed it into the glass container. The container shattered. The cork fell onto the floor. I placed the cork into a ziplock bag, blew the candle out, then turned off the lamp. I snuck out of the church, safely back to my mother's car.

I couldn't sleep that night, checking the cork on my bedside table every five minutes.

I'd already secured a buyer, a guy I'd sold meth to a few years back.

We met under an old oak tree at a park the following morning. I handed him the zip lock bag while pretending to tie my shoelaces.

"Nobody's watching us, Billy. Stand up, would you!? Let's see what you got." He removed his dark shades. "This thing's nice. I think I can shop it. You got the papers?"

"What papers?"

"Authentication! How do we know it's real?"

"The priest said it is, told me himself."

The man laughed. Then his face tightened. "A priest says a lot of things. You wasting my time, Billy. I can't help you if I don't have the papers."

He shoved the bag into my hand and turned for the parking lot.

I thought about breaking into the church again that night to look for the papers. But despite the itch worsening, I wasn't willing to take the risk. I waited three days to let the dust settle.

The time passed without Father Sampson's daily call. I wondered if he'd figured it out, giving me space to fess up before he called the cops.

I felt ready to take a crack at finding the papers. To fix the itch. Walking into the Wednesday mass service ten minutes late, I noticed a different priest behind the altar, a much older man. In the front pew, I immediately recognized the man with the skull tattoo and the pacing-in-circles lady. My heart beat a hundred miles through all the Hail Marys, then a hundred miles faster at the

end of the benediction. I waited until most of the con-
gregation had left. I approached the old priest as he
headed into the vestry. The skull-tattoo man and the
lady were already in the room when I entered.

"Father, where's Father Sampson?" I said.

"Nobody told you?"

"Told me what?"

"Some massive insurance payout came through for
him, so he quit- packed up everything in a day. Headed
somewhere warm, I think."

The priest moved to the windowsill, fetched the key
underneath the violet, and opened the cabinet.

"I heard about that stolen cork. Such a pity." I stepped
closer, in front of the skull-tattoo man, trying to peer
into the cabinet underneath the priest's drooping shoulders.

"What cork?" The priest said.

"The one from when the pope visited."

"Jesus of Nazareth, Son of God..." The woman
screamed.

The priest chuckled, then turned his head and squinted at me. "The pope?"

"Father Sampson said he was here a few months
ago."

"Told me that cork was worth the price of five of
these churches at least."

The priest's chuckle grew into a belly laugh. "That
Father Sampson sure had a sense of humor. I'll give
him that! You got a better chance at seeing Jesus himself around here than the pope, my son!"

My eyes moved to the collection plate. "Say, Father, are you still keeping the church key under the lemon tree outside? Father Sampson would leave it there so I could come and pray during the off hours."

"For me too," the skull tattoo man said, as his eyes focused on the collection plate.

The priest locked the cabinet and returned the key underneath the violet. "Strictly against church policy, my children. I'm quite surprised to learn he let you do that."

I didn't say goodbye to the priest, hurrying out of the church with the man and the lady.

"Can I catch a ride, kid?" The tattoo man put his big hand on my shoulder.

"Sure."

I turned the key in the ignition. The lady started banging on my window.

"Forget her," the man said. "Just drive."

We stopped at a red light. The man turned his head to look at me. "He told you about the cork too, didn't he?"

I said nothing.

"The thing I'm trying to figure out is how he convinced the insurance company to insure that piece of shit."

"Did you ever see Father Sampson with a lady?" I said, noticing the man starting to scratch himself.

"Many times. That's why they called him Sampson, I reckon."

I turned up the radio.

"I think you can fit through the bars of that window, kid. There's probably a grand in that offering plate, you know? What do you say?"

I dropped the man off at a nearby soup kitchen, shaking his hand before saying goodbye. "I'll pick you up tonight."

I scratched all the way home, unafraid of drawing any blood.

Do or Die

"Our facility's brand-spanking new! Home to the highest rollers in the world—private jet, caviar, and crabs for lunch kinda folks. You got to get a piece of this, son!"

The general manger slurred his words on the phone.

"Seems like the opportunity of a lifetime, Mr. Bellingham. I'd love to accept the position!"

On the way home from work, I bought a bottle of champagne.

"What's the occasion?" Kate said, setting a plate of spaghetti and meatballs before me.

"You're not going to believe it."

She moved her chair closer, grabbing my hand. "They offered you the job? You're not serious?"

"I told you, babe. Didn't I?"

We packed up our things that night, laughing and crying, then spent our last dime on two one-way tickets to the Mojave Desert.

On my first day, Mr. Bellingham introduced me to most of the staff and gave me a thorough tour of the state-of-the-art facility. I tried to resist testing the fancy water dispensers and tasting the complimentary snacks in the fridge drawers.

We finished the tour in the soon-to-be-opened casino. The red, blue, and yellow ceiling lights appeared as great pillars shining onto the shadowed card tables and empty bars.

"Well, what do you think of the place, Jim?" Mr. Bellingham pulled out two chairs from a blackjack table.

I set my package of spiced nuts on my thigh, munching quickly, brushing my hand over my lips. "This place is incredible. How does it get any better?"

Mr. Bellingham held out his hand, furling his walrus mustache with his other. "Welcome to the team! We have high hopes for you!"

He pulled a stack of papers from a folder he'd been carrying.

"Here's the contract, the usual BS you read in these kinds of things. Just sign here."

Icon Reserve; Director of Pickleball; Salary with commission; Two Weeks PTO; 401K; Medical insurance; Daily lunch.

I scanned the four-page document in less than ten seconds and signed the appropriate boxes.

"Now, there's just one more thing I must make you aware of. Just a formality in case HR ever asks you about it."

I held the tip of the black ballpoint pen on the date section. "What's that, Mr. Bellingham?"

"Call me, Randy, son. Please."

Randy cupped his palm over my shoulder and squeezed. "How good are you at Pickleball anyway?"

"Well, when I was competing…."

"So you're good," Randy interrupted.

"Yeah, you could say that."

"Well, HR isn't too fond of gambling with the members. And there's a lot of that happening around here. So I'll just leave it that. But maybe you and I can talk later once you've familiarized yourself with the place and our membership. We'll get drinks and watch some dancing girls. You into that kind of thing?"

I smiled nervously, unsure how to respond.

"I won't have a problem with gambling, don't worry." Handing the contract to Randy, I gripped his sweaty hand and shook it again.

"It'll be the best decision you ever made," Randy crumpled the contract into his file. He slapped my back and pressed into the top of my neck with the tips of his fingers.

The following day, my first actual day on the job, I met with the concierge staff to review the type of pickleball programming I planned on introducing.

The lead concierge, a bob-cut, tanned skin, glitter finger-nailed type gal, paused her reading of my list of offerings at *Beat the Pro*.

"What exactly is Beat the Pro?" She smiled.

I noticed Randy behind us, looking up from his computer screen.

I made sure to speak loudly. "It's going to help grow the program significantly. Beat the Pro was one of my old club's most popular offerings. If a member or guest beats me, they play for free. If they lose, they pay. It's not a timed event, so you can really make a decent buck on it if you play your cards right at seventy dollars per set."

"Oh, interesting," the lady replied, twirling her hair with a pen.

"You ever lose, Jimbo?" Randy exclaimed, standing and sliding out from his desk.

"Never," I said, feeling the bright glow of pride settle on my face.

Randy caught up with me as I left the concierge, slinging his arm around my shoulder. "I think I got your first customer. This Beat the Pro is just his sort of thing. He's some kind of a pickle expert with a wicked serve, I hear. Let me call him. We'll meet at the courts around 9 am tomorrow. That work for you?"

I felt a flutter of nerves. "Sure thing, boss. Sounds fun."

That night I iced my knees, prepped my bag with athletic tape and extra socks, and skipped my usual beer.

"I haven't seen you this nervous since that tournament you played in last year," Kate said as she kissed me goodnight.

"I have a Beat the Pro tomorrow against one of the better playing members."

"That's where you stand to make a lot of money if you beat him quickly, right?"

"Yeah, upwards of $300 for the hour."

Kate kissed me again, but this time on the lips.

When I arrived at work the following morning, I jumped on the stationary bike until I broke a sweat. I wrapped my ankles and powdered my hands.

"Jimmy, meet Jeff." Randy walked into the small court-side gym with his arm around a short, stocky man with quads bigger than my head.

"So you're the new pickle pro? You any good?"

I couldn't see Jeff's eyes through his dark-tinted shades. I waited for him to remove them as we shook hands, but he didn't.

I felt jittery as I spoke, babbling. "Yeah, I'm just happy to be here. So eager to grow the program, you know? Ready to break a sweat?"

Randy slung his arms around our necks, then pulled us in close. "Let's get the show on the road, gentleman. Vegas got Jimbo as a two-point favorite in this one." Randy let out a deep belly laugh, to which I responded with a manufactured giggle. Jeff stood straight-faced and stiff.

As we warmed up, I felt my feet settle into my shoes when I noticed a weakness in Jeff's game. He used the same side of the paddle to hit his backhand as his forehand, an elementary mistake that would cost him time in a quick exchange. After a standard five-minute warm-up, Randy shouted from behind the fence, "Okay, let's get this going, boys!"

"Serves?" I asked, loading my paddle as though to hit the ball.

"No serves," Jeff replied with a cold, serious tone. "I'll start."

I heard the thump of rubber to plastic before I could set my feet. Jeff's serve had an unusual side spin, but nothing too complicated I couldn't handle. I drove the return up the line to his backhand, tailing my shot and approaching the net. He twisted his paddle, swinging, but the ball was already behind him, bumping against the fence for a clean winner.

Randy howled, clapping and jumping in place. "Too much heat for you on that one, Jeffy Boy!"

Randy approached me on a water break after I'd won two sets without Jeff earning a single point, "Make this set close, kid. It'll be good for business."

I nodded, feeling the claws of my competitive spirit gnash against the thought of tanking a few shots. I gave Jeff nine points, hiding my discomfort with a warm smile.

We shook hands. Jeff removed his shades, handing me two hundred and ten dollars. He stared long into my eyes. "You're a hell of a player, kid; glad to have you here. But you shouldn't have taken it easy on me during that final set."

I walked off the court buzzed, nervous, and with a slight stutter in my step. The three of us sat in the shaded area and sipped on water.

"You almost got that last set, Jeffy Boy. We'll have to run it back with a big crowd? What do you say?"

"Sure, why not." Jeff said.

When Randy changed the subject and began speaking about all the famous people he'd had dinner with recently, Jeff got up.

"You did good, kid. Hell of a player."

"Thanks, Jeff," I said, smiling.

We watched Jeff get into his Lincoln Navigator.

"You and I can do good things here if we play our cards right."

I scanned the area, marveling at the facility's sheen, the bright paint on the courts and the building, and the beautifully manicured landscape.

"I truly believe we can," I said with a big grin.

Randy lowered his voice, eyes circling as though afraid of somebody hearing him.

"Some high roller execs are coming in this weekend. They love betting against Jeff, love seeing him lose. And they bring a great crowd. I'm going to let these rich boys know how badly you walloped Jeff, then tell them Jeff thinks he can beat you, that he wants a re-match. And then you're going to play him again on Saturday, and you're going to lose."

I jerked backward in my seat. "What?"

"Yeah, you heard me."

"You want me to lose? To Jeff? In front of a bunch of high-profile people? How's that going to make me look?"

"Now, now. Settle down. I like it. You're competitive. You got drive. That's great. But listen, the payout's going to be worth it." Randy turned his eyes to the bills sticking out of my pocket.

"Fifty times more than what you just scored. Call it a sign-on bonus if you want. Two months pay for a little Saturday morning pickleball match. But you have to lose. You're fired if you don't."

The glow on Randy's leathered, sun-burned face disappeared as though he'd taken off a mask. What lay underneath was a wrinkled old man with dark purple patches underneath his black-as-night eyes.

"Fired?" I said in shock.

"It's not personal, kid. You've got nothing to lose here. Just think about how happy you're going to make your little lady with all that cash. Don't be caught behind the eight-ball on this one."

I sat silent, not meeting Randy's eyes.

"I'll need to sleep on it." I said after a while. "I'm not sure I'm that type of guy, honestly."

Bursting to his feet, Randy massaged his hand into my neck, squeezing the tight spots. "What's there to sleep on? You show up Saturday and lose, or you never show up again."

Images of Kate flashed across my mind as Randy delivered a final squeeze and walked away. He shot a finger gun at me, smiling wickedly.

I cracked open a cold beer as I sat down for dinner that night.

"So we're celebrating?"

"Celebrating what?" I quickly replied.

"Your win today? I'm guessing you won? Although that look on your face tells me otherwise."

"Oh yes, that beat the pro match. Yes, I won that."

"How much you make?"

"Two hundred and ten dollars."

Kate got up from her chair. She wrapped her arms around me. "How did I get so lucky to find you?"

I kissed her on the cheek.

"What's bothering you, Jim?" She pulled back.

"He wants me to lose on Saturday."

Her forehead creased into a frown. "Who?"

"Randy, my boss."

"Why?"

"He's got a side bet with some big wigs coming into town."

Kate sat back down. "What's in it for you?"

"Ten K."

"Say what!?" Kate sprung to her feet.

"I'm not doing it. I won't, Kate."

She came closer to me again. "For ten thousand dollars? C'mon, babe, let's get real here! That's life-changing money for us right now! And you'll just be doing what your boss wants you to do anyway!"

"No! My reputation is not for sale!"

I downed my beer, then put my plate in the sink. I wasn't going to tell Kate that Randy would fire me if I didn't comply.

"You need to think long and hard about this, Jim. Seriously."

"I got us this far, didn't I? My decision is final."

Kate pestered me numerous times before Saturday, urging me to "lay my pride aside" and to "think about us."

I couldn't sleep all week.

On Saturday, I clocked in as the first kiss of light touched the desert landscape. The maintenance team had set up three four-row bleachers around the pickleball court. Thirty minutes later, the facility began buzzing with more people than I'd seen during my first week on the job.

Randy spilled his coffee, slapping me on my back when I walked onto the court. "Go get 'em, kid." I turned to see him sit down on one of the top rows amongst a group of men wearing cowboy hats and glistening gold watches.

Winning the coin toss, I elected to serve. I attempted an extremely aggressive shot, hoping the ball would sail out, but it skimmed the line, causing the crowd to gasp in awe. I tried it again. Jeff got in the way this time, and the ball hit his shoe. On the third point, I floated the serve, allowing Jeff to hit a decent approach shot and come in for a winning volley. Watching the ball fly past me, then listening to the loud clapping and cheering, made my stomach sink. I couldn't look at the faces on the bleachers, afraid seeing them would make me change my mind. Tied up at four points a piece in the first set, I began closing my eyes before every point, painting Kate's smile across the blank canvas of my mind. Five minutes later, Jeff had the first set eleven to five, the crowd chanting his name.

I put my towel over my head and poured out a bottle of water on myself.

"Hey, kid," Jeff nudged me, whispering.

I lifted a small corner of the towel to look at him.

"Let's go take a bathroom break."

"I don't need one," I said.

"Yeah, you do. Let's go."

I waited until Jeff exited the court. He stopped at the gate, looked at Randy, lifted his shades, and stared at me until I stood and followed him.

The bathroom door slammed shut behind me, Jeff bolting it before anybody else could enter.

"Whatever he's paying you, it ain't worth your reputation, kid."

"What do you mean," I clamored, not looking Jeff in the eyes.

"C'mon. You might be fooling all those people out there, but not me. I know what's going on. I've known Randy for a long time. Long before this place ever existed. You're a shell of the player I faced the other day. Please don't insult my intelligence. And don't insult my pride by letting me beat you. What's he paying you?"

"It's not about the money."

Jeff stepped closer. "It's always about the money."

"He said I'd lose my job if I didn't tank. Do or die."

Jeff smacked his hand against the wall. "That son of a…"

He tugged on the bathroom door, double-checking he'd locked it. "I know those businessmen he's sitting with. They love betting against me, but I've got a good relationship with them. You're going to let me get seven points ahead, and then I'll text my buddy and tell him to triple what he's put on you. Randy won't be able to resist. And then you're going to do your damnedest to beat me. But I ain't backing down. If I win, I'll spot the cash. If you win, we run Randy out of town. You hear me?"

My eyes fell to the tiled floor. "What about my job? I got a wife."

"You ain't listening, kid. You beat me, and Randy's gone. There's no way he's coming up with all that cash. He'll duck and run like the cheat he is. And if I win, you get one hell of a signing bonus."

I didn't need a second more to think about it. I shook Jeff's hand, waited for him to take the court, then followed, ready to begin the second set. Jeff raced to a seven-point lead as I handed him errors and floating shots to demolish. Before calling out the score, Jeff requested another bathroom break, which I obliged. I watched him grab his phone, sling it into his pocket, then exit the court. I put my towel over my head and closed my eyes, imagining that the match was just getting started. Then I scanned the crowd, catching the eyes of a few people. Sitting near Randy, one of the men wearing a cowboy hat began mouthing something at me, slowly raising his beer. Jeff interrupted my studying of the man, planting his feet on the baseline, bouncing the ball on his paddle, shouting, "You ready, kid?"

I didn't care now that I looked like a completely different player as I screamed through the second set, putting Jeff on training wheels.

The crowd was silent as I began serving for the third and final set. I looked up to find Randy before striking the ball. He wasn't sitting near the executives anymore. As I continued to search the sea of faces, I heard that familiar scratchy voice behind me, "I hope you know what you're doing here. Don't be a fool now." Randy was leaning up against the fence. I felt a nervous chill run through my hands as I was about to serve, but that quickly disappeared when Jeff shouted from across the net, "C'mon, kid, I don't have all day!"

I went up eight zero, soaking up the crowd's energy, occasionally looking back at Randy. He was pacing back and forth behind me, mumbling threats.

At 10-0, I yelled, "Match point!."

Randy burst onto the court, shouting, "It's fixed! It's all a scam. This ain't right what you're doing. The both of you! We're calling it a tie!"

"The hell we are!" Jeff shouted, removing his shades and walking towards Randy. "Serve, kid!"

Ignoring Jeff, Randy turned to face me. "You're fired! Get out of here!"

One of the men with the big cowboy hat, who'd mouthed something earlier to me, stood up and made his way to the court. Then, perching his elbows on the fence calmly, relaxedly, he said, "Randy, if you don't let these men finish this match, I'll make sure this is the last club you ever work at."

At once, without a word, Randy left the court and made his way toward the man with the cowboy hat. He began speaking to him, shoulders hunched, head dipping. I tried to listen, moving closer, but Jeff shouted again, "Let's go, kid! I ain't got all day!"

Jeff positioned himself a little off the court, hiding his backhand, leaving the center line wide open. I softened my grip, then swung faster than I had all morning, snapping my wrist at the last minute, giving the ball a little side spin. The serve skimmed an inch above the net, painting the middle line, leaving Jeff flat-footed and out of position. Ace. Set. Match.

We shook hands while the crowd stood to their feet and applauded. A deafening screech blared from the parking lot as we turned to watch Randy's red Mustang blaze toward the I-40.

Maybe It's Not Too Late

We fell out of love in a hurry that night. Suzy flipped over my dirty ashtray and tossed my empty beer can at me while I lay sprawled on the sofa watching the game. "You can't just keep feeling sorry for yourself, Barry. Bad shit happens. To everybody. All the time."

It'd been five years since the car crash. I came out of it unscathed, but our youngest child, Anthony, got crushed. It wasn't my fault. Suzy never blamed me once. But I hadn't gone a day without replaying the accident, imagining what I could've done differently.

Suzy yanked the remote out of my hand, then turned off the TV. "I've had enough, Barry! I can't keep doing this. Me and the kids deserve more."

I ignored her. I'd been ignoring her for five years.

I stood up to turn the TV back on and noticed a different sadness in Suzy's eyes. She touched my wrist. "I'm going to my mom's. I'll be back tomorrow evening to fetch the kids. Make the most of your time. You won't be seeing them for a while."

I stubbed my toe into the leg of the living room table, then turned up the volume on the TV.

The kids were fast asleep when I leaned up against our cold living room window, watching Suzy speed away in her beat-up Buick. I grabbed my carton of Marlboro reds and a close-to-empty lighter. As I lit the cigarette, Danny, my youngest, let out a cry, a kind of cry that I couldn't ignore. I stabbed the cigarette into the kitchen counter, then threw the whole pack into the trash can. My baby boy had his little foot caught in the railing of his crib. "It's okay, Daniel," I said quietly, careful not to wake the girls, maneuvering his foot back onto his blanket. He rolled over and went back to sleep. Instead of tip-toeing out of the room, I lay there next to him with my hand in his, patting his backside with the other.

I was still beside Danny's crib when the morning light hit my eyes. I rushed to the kitchen while all the kids remained asleep. Half an hour later, Sam, my oldest, walked in for breakfast. Observing a pile of chocolate pancakes on a plate, her eyebrows rose. "What's this? Where's mom?"

"You can have as much whipped cream as you want!"

Daniel and Katie followed hand in hand.

"Chocolate pancakes! My favorite!" Katie yelled. She grabbed the aerosol can and began molding mountains of white whipped cream on a plate of pancakes. All three looked at me with giant eyes of surprise when little Katie lost control and made a huge mess on the kitchen table. I forced a grin.

"I'm sorry, Daddy," little Katie said with a soft, fearful look.

"It's okay, baby," I whispered.

Katie tightened her hand around my finger, studying my eyes. "What's wrong, Daddy?"

"She's gone. Your mommy. She's gone."

"Why?" Sam said, frowning.

"I don't know."

Katie's eyes filled with tears. She jumped into my arms, howling with her face buried into my chest.

"Something happened between you two, didn't it?" Sam yelled. Her eyes looked like tiny daggers.

"We're going for a drive after breakfast. Get everything you need."

"I'm not going without Mom!" Sam shouted.

*

I watched Sam, barely ten, strap baby Dan into his car seat. "You got those straps tight enough?"

"Yes, Dad. I've done this a thousand times."

I handed Katie my phone so she could watch YouTube videos.

"You're breaking the rule, Dad," Sam barked as I reversed the station wagon from the driveway.

"What rule?"

"Mom won't allow us to watch YouTube without first telling her one thing we're grateful for."

"I don't remember that?"

"Of course you don't."

"Well, I suppose that's a good enough rule to keep."

"Why?" Katie lifted her head, taking a break from the phone to look at me.

The wagon idled as I shifted it into neutral. "Well, I suppose it's important to get into the habit of being thankful. Makes us think about the good instead of the bad."

"Like, why mom's leaving you?" Sam said in a low, sad voice.

I moved my eyes between all three of them. It felt like I was seeing my children for the first time, observing new things. Dan was asleep, mouth open. His little tongue was trapped to the roof of his mouth as though somebody was holding a finger underneath it. Did he always sleep like that? Katie had a small brown mole above her left eye and a tuft of blonde hair growing out of it. And Sam's cold blue eyes had these tiny green lines around her pupils I'd never noticed.

"Why are you looking at me like that?" Sam said irritably.

"Because I love you." I put my hand on her knee and squeezed. She jerked her leg from my grip, saying nothing. She pressed her face against the window, pretending to watch a dog gnaw on a bone.

I felt a sinking feeling in my stomach as we drove through the neighborhood, remembering the first day we'd found our house. At the time, we'd been renting down the street and wanted something bigger. I'd seen a for sale sign on the way home from work. One night, after dinner, we went on a family walk. Suzy grabbed my hand as we sprinted up the steps leading to the porch. "Can we?" she said, her eyes bright and full of hope. We put an offer on it the next day.

"Glad I'm not there today," Sam mumbled. She stared at a group of kids playing on the playground as we passed her school.

"I thought you loved school?"

"Not even a little. I guess that's something to be thankful for, right?" Her eyes remained jagged.

"We're going to have a good day today." I smiled.

"Good? Like maybe you'll pretend to give a shit?"

I wanted to stop the car and squirt hand sanitizer onto Sam's tongue. Or hug her. I couldn't decide. Instead, I kept driving, not saying anything. Sam's eyes narrowed further, and then she looked away, slumping into the window again so I couldn't see her in the mirror.

I felt a soft touch on my shoulder. "It's okay, Daddy," Katie whispered. She set my phone on the middle console. "I love you."

"Maybe we can find a park. How does that sound?"

Katie squeezed my hand. "Can we go to Disneyland?"

I laughed.

I kept staring at Sam, hoping to see a smile unravel on her face. Daniel began crying hysterically. We all turned our attention to him.

"What's wrong?" I asked.

"He's hungry. He always gets like this when he's hungry. Did you pack any of those baby snacks for him?" Sam said with a matter-of-fact tone.

"What baby snacks?"

"Underneath the sink. The wafers and animal crackers."

"I didn't even know we had those."

Sighing, Sam gave Daniel her finger and let him chew on it. "We need to stop and get him something to eat."

I turned off the interstate following a sign for a 7-Eleven.

"Daddy, can we get some white frosted donuts and a slushy?" Katie curled around my seat, staring at me with soft puppy eyes, blinking rapidly.

"Of course, my girl!" I rubbed her head. She quickly retreated.

"Mom would never let us do that." Sam pulled her finger out of Daniel's mouth and replaced it with another.

"Eat donuts?" I said with a surprised tone.

"It's like you've been living on a different planet. She always says 'something healthy before something unhealthy', not the other way around."

"Well, I guess that's a good rule, too."

When we pulled into the parking lot, Sam had taken her finger out of Daniel's mouth, and he was crying again. I jumped out of the driver's seat and raced around the car to unhook Daniel from his car seat. But Sam had already taken care of it, stepping out of the vehicle, securing Daniel on her hip, and bouncing him.

"He likes that," I said, touching Sam's shoulder. She looked like a small crooked tree standing with Daniel; her buckling right hip held all their weight.

"I can take him now," I said, reaching toward Daniel. Upon seeing me, Daniel immediately turned away, tunneling his little head into Sam's chest.

"He likes me." She said. "I got him."

"Does a frozen waffle count?" Katie gripped my hand, leading me into the store.

"That seems healthy enough, doesn't it, my little girl?"

"Katie!" Sam yelled.

"Well, Mom isn't here!"

I watched Katie's eyes grow heavy with tears as she tried holding them back, her little lip quivering uncontrollably.

I wrapped my arms around her. "It's okay, my girl. We can get anything you want."

She kept crying. "It's okay, my girl. It's okay."

She buried her face into my stomach, soaking my shirt with her tears. "Are you and Mommy going to get a divorce?"

Sam tapped Katie on the arm and said, "Look, they have your favorite kind." Katie lifted her face from my stomach. Wiping her eyes, she resumed her cheery disposition as though she hadn't shed a single tear.

I bent and whispered in Sam's ear. "That was sweet of you. Thank you."

As the shop attendant rang up the waffles, donuts, and Daniel's crackers, I suddenly realized we'd bought nothing for Sam.

"Just a minute. Sorry." I said to the man behind the register.

"Sam, go get something for yourself."

"I'm not hungry." She stood with folded arms, not looking at me in the eyes.

"Sam, please. You'll be hungry later."

Sam and Daniel exited the shop. I grabbed Katie's hand, "Go get a snack for your sister. Something she'll like."

We got back on the interstate. I turned down the 80s music playing on the radio. I readjusted the mirror. "I don't want you girls to worry about Mommy and me. Okay?"

"So you aren't getting a divorce?" Katie turned to look at Sam with a wide smile.

"They are," Sam muttered.

I felt my face tighten.

Sam continued, "When was the last time you sat down for dinner with us, Dad? Or took us to school? Or helped us with our homework? Or put us to bed? Not once since Anthony died!"

"Now you listen here…"

"Hey, look!" Katie shouted.

We followed her eyes and pointed finger. Suzy's favorite park was up ahead.

"It's mom's happy place!" Katie said excitedly.

"Want to go play a quick game of tag!?" I said, trying to dissolve the tension between Sam and me.

"Can we?" Katie poked her head around my seat, rubbing it up and down my elbow.

"What do you say, Sam? Feel like losing to an old man?"

Sam turned her face so I couldn't see her gaze. But I noticed her lips raised ever so slightly, and a few small lines ran down her eyes.

"I can see that smile you're trying to hide, you know."

She hid her face further.

When I turned left into the park, both girls unbuckled their seat belts and shifted to the edge of their seats.

The walking path weaved through a cluster of big white oak trees. To either side of the trail, people had planted little flowers in pots with notes sticking out of the soil. Suzy's favorite was a pot with a violet that always seemed to be struggling, leaves flaking with a touch and yellowish purple petals. The violet had a note that read, "If you aren't making it today, wait for tomorrow."

Sam walked up to the flower, observing it for a minute. She turned around, looking at me like she'd forgotten something. She tapped me on the shoulder, then sprinted towards the weed-ridden field. "Tag, you're it!"

"Here, Katie, look after Daniel." I put little Dan into Katie's arms, then took off after Sam. "Here I come!" My knees crunched and creaked with every strained stride, looking back to ensure Katie and Dan were okay. Sam moved faster than I remembered and cut with a dancer's grace. I cornered her near an old soccer goal with a missing net. "Nowhere to go now, is there?"

She giggled. I stutter-stepped left then right, Sam in sync with my every move as though we were tied to each other by a string. I leaped forward and screamed, clutching the back of my leg, and falling to the ground.

"Dad, are you okay?" Sam moved closer, extending her hand.

I snatched her hand, then pulled her quickly into my stomach, "Got you, little girl!"

She squirmed in and out of my tickles, laughing, jamming her bony elbows into my side. I wrapped my arms around her, squeezing tight enough that she couldn't move. She fought me for a while, then dropped back into my chest like a baby falling asleep. I rubbed her shoulders, not saying anything. Just when I thought Sam might turn her head up at me and smile, she began to sob, burying her nose into my sleeve.

"What's wrong, my girl?" I tried pulling her from my chest to see her face, but she wouldn't let me. Her arms closed around me and held me so tightly that I could feel her bony fingers dig into my skin. "Tell me, Sam. Please, my girl. What is it?"

Her muffled screams echoed into my sternum. "Where have you been? I've only ever wanted my daddy. But now it's too late. You've ripped us apart!"

"Look at me, Sam, please!" I shouted, desperately trying to unclench her. I began to cry slowly, tears barely big enough to roll down my cheeks. Suddenly, my whole body went limp. It felt like someone was ripping the skin from my stomach, exposing my insides. I squeezed Sam, wailing, dripping my tears onto her thick, brown, matted hair. I didn't see her lift her head, but I felt it. I sensed her looking at me, but I was too ashamed to look back at her. I wanted to run away, the only thing I'd been good at since the car crash.

"Mom," Sam whispered.

"Mom." She said again, louder. "Look, Dad!"

Rubbing my sleeves into my eyes, I turned around with Sam still in my arms. With a violet in her hair,

Suzy walked towards us, Danny on her hip, Katie holding her hand.

"Maybe it's not too late, Dad." Sam jumped out of my arms and raced towards her mother.

Mr. Butterfly Man

"He fired Rex," Jimmy whispered, setting a stack of papers on my desk.

"No way!?" I hit save on the document I was typing, lifting my gaze to make eye contact. "There's no one better than Rex. What the hell happened?"

Jimmy looked over my shoulder, moving his pen haphazardly on a financial report. "For being too cocky. That's what Shandy told me."

I followed Jimmy's eyes to Mr. Sizemore's office. "Damn, I guess everybody really is replaceable."

"There's something not right about it."

"What do you mean?"

Sizemore's door opened. Shooting up as though electrocuted, then quickly easing back down, Jimmy leaned over into my workspace, speaking much louder. "It's off, Martin. I'm telling you. By half a percentage point."

A hand squeezed my shoulder. "I take it you two heard about Rex?"

"Good morning, Mr. Sizemore," I said, casually peering back over my shoulder.

"No." Jimmy replied, "But you know what they say about Eagles fans."

"What?" Mr. Sizemore asked, a boom in his voice.

"Well, I don't really know," Jimmy managed. "You're an Eagles fan, Mr. Sizemore?"

"He was too cocky. He's been on a high horse for a while now. I don't care if you can sell life insurance to a baby. If you don't know how to step in line when I ask you to, then we're going to have a problem."

Mr. Sizemore removed a folder from under his armpit. "You know what that means for the both of you, don't you?"

"Commission raise?" I said, smiling.

Sizemore's eyebrows stressed into a V shape.

"Step in line when you ask us?"

Sizemore placed the folder on my desk.

One hand on Jimmy's shoulder, another on mine, Sizemore squeezed. "You're going to take over all of Rex's accounts. You hear?"

"You won't be hiring a replacement?" Jimmy stepped back out from under Mr. Sizemore's hand, a slight quivering in his voice.

"You want to make money, don't you? That's why you took the job, right? That's why I hired you, correct? That's why you showed up today, isn't it?" Sizemore straightened, towering almost half a head over Jimmy.

"Yes, yes, of course, Sir," Jimmy said.

"Then get back to work. The both of you."

Sizemore walked back to his office but turned around just before opening his door. "There's one more thing I want you both to do."

"What is it, boss?" Jimmy asked.

"Meet me at The Corner Pocket for a beer after work. You know the place, right?"

Jimmy and I gave each other a puzzled look.

"Well, do you?" Sizemore barked.

"Yes, yes, a beer sounds great, Mr. Sizemore. We'll see you there." I said quickly.

"Looking forward to it!" Jimmy added.

*

Walking through the faded blue saloon doors, I stopped at the threshold, doing a double take. I spotted Rex under a neon pink lamp at the far end of the room. He was sitting across from a long-haired brunette woman whose face I couldn't make out. I lowered my gaze, looking for a table that was out of Rex's line of sight.

"Is that who I think it is?"

Jimmy pushed his hand into the small of my back, moving me forward. "Yeah, what are the chances? No sign of Sizemore. This should be interesting."

"Let's go sit over there," I whispered, turning towards the table I'd already marked.

Sitting across from each other, Jimmy and I could see Rex and his girl with little difficulty.

"Don't look now, Marty, but you know who that lady is with him?" Jimmy grabbed my hand, squeezing.

He wiggled to the end of his seat, craning his neck. "That's Sizemore's wife!"

I followed Jimmy's movement.

"What?" I couldn't not look at her.

"He's bonking her, Marty. Damn."

"Are you sure that's her?" I strained my eyes, lowering my head under the pink light.

"Yeah, I'm positive. I'd never forget that hook nose! I met her at the Christmas party two years ago."

"Do you know what you want?" A waitress approached our table.

We squirmed back to the middle of our seats, grabbing the paper menus.

"We're still waiting on someone," I said, looking at my watch.

"Just bring two beers for now, would you?" Jimmy said, peering around the pink-skirted waitress' bulgy hips.

"What kind of beers?"

"Whatever you…"

"We'll take two Heinekens," I said.

"I bet Sizemore walked in here, saw the two of them, then walked back out." Jimmy kept staring.

Moving to the end of our seats again, we watched Rex and Sizemore's wife hold hands across the table. They took a final sip from their drinks, then stood and headed for the exit.

"We've got to follow them," Jimmy whispered, his eyes glowing.

"For what?"

Jimmy slid off the black leather seat, reaching for his phone in his pocket.

"Jimmy!"

When I caught up to Jimmy, he was kneeling behind a red SUV, with his phone's camera locked on Rex and

Sizemore's wife kissing. Rex squeezed her into his chest, then they got into separate vehicles and drove away in opposite directions.

"You think Sizemore's known about this for a while?"

"Of course, he knows," I said. "Why else do you fire your number one salesman?"

"You fellas gonna pay for your beers?"

I stood up, showing my wallet to our waitress. "Coming, ma'am."

When we sat back in our seats, Jimmy raised the menu to the side of his face, then whispered to the big-hipped waitress, "Say, ma'am, did you see that couple sitting over there?"

"You mean Rex and Tania?"

"Yeah, you see them in here often?"

"They just recently started coming here. You boys getting anything to eat?"

"No, thanks," I said, sipping on my Heineken. "Just beer tonight."

Jimmy's eyes went big. "I can't believe this shit."

*

I ate a big bite of my peanut butter and jelly sandwich, noticing Mr. Sizemore placing a chair next to me.

"So, how are those accounts looking? You manage to call everybody and explain the situation?" He removed the plastic wrapper of what looked like a day's old chicken salad.

I dramatized my chewing motion, pointing to my cheek.

"Mr. Sizemore. We missed you at The Corner Pocket last night." Jimmy placed his hand on Sizemore's shoulder and sat in the open chair on the other side.

"Yeah, sorry about that. I had something to take care of. So you ended up going, though? How was it?"

"A pretty standard evening, I'd say," Jimmy smiled at me.

There was a short silence.

"You won't believe who we ran into." I set my sandwich down.

"Rex! Can you believe that!?" Jimmy shouted.

Sizemore dropped his fork into his salad. "What? Was he alone?"

"He was with a woman."

Sizemore stood up. "About this tall? Bob cut, brown hair, hook nose? You ever meet my wife?"

I spoke before Jimmy had a chance. "Can't be too sure. But yeah, I think she had brown hair. I don't believe we've met your wife before." I shot Jimmy a quick wink.

Sizemore put a hand on each of our shoulders. "You boys go there a lot? To The Corner Pocket?"

"Not really," I said, biting into my sandwich again.

"You're going to keep going there after work, you hear me. You're going to take photos for me. Of Rex and that woman. Take a video now and again if you can."

"Well, actually…"

I flashed Jimmy a death stare.

"Yes, Mr. Sizemore, carry on," I said. "What is it that you want?"

"I want evidence!" Sizemore slammed his hand on the desk. There was an awkward silence. He moved his eyes throughout the rest of the lunchroom.

"There's something I've suspected for a long time now. It'll just give me a little validation. That's all. Just keep going to that bar. Hell, you can leave work early if you have to. If you see him with that woman, any woman, document it. You hear me?"

"Can we stay on the clock?" Jimmy asked.

Sizemore didn't hear him; his back had already turned, and he was walking away from us towards his office.

Jimmy flung his hands into the air when Sizemore's office door closed. "Why'd you stop me like that?"

I craned my neck to look at Sizemore's door, then turned back to face Jimmy. "Because if we play our cards right, we'll make out with way more than a little commission raise here. But we got to get more footage and recorded conversations. We got to get the whole damn gamut of this affair. When we present it to Sizemore, he'll have to have it. He'll pay us far more than what he'd be willing to pay us today for the little we have."

Jimmy slapped me on the back. I coughed up a bit of my sandwich. "Brilliant, Marty! Damn brilliant!"

*

An hour before our usual clock-out time, Sizemore scampered out of his office. "Why are the both of you still here?"

I looked at Jimmy.

"I bet that rat bastard's already downed two beers by now!"

We remained blank-faced.

"Corner Pocket!" Sizemore tapped his watch. "It's time for you to go! Collect everything you can on that cocky son of a bitch!"

When we walked into The Corner Pocket, my eyes immediately went to the table Rex and Tania had been sitting at the day before. "Damn it," I mumbled. "Empty."

"Look," Jimmy nudged my shoulder.

I followed his gaze and noticed Rex and Tania at a table closer to the bar, in a far less discreet location of the room.

"I think the bar will give us our best vantage point." Jimmy stepped ahead, grabbing a stool directly behind Rex's table.

The bar was double-sided. We camouflaged behind two dark brown counters and two overhead rows of upside-down liquor bottles.

"Can I get your biggest mug, please?"

"Mug of what?" the barman said to Jimmy.

"I just want the mug."

"Miller light. Make it two," I said quickly.

As the barman poured our beers, I noticed Jimmy removing his phone from his pocket.

"Don't get caught," I whispered. "We've got to do this slow and steady."

Jimmy leaned his phone up against his mug of Miller Lite. He bent his neck awkwardly to look at the screen.

"Got it?" I asked.

"It's perfect." He smiled.

We were on our last sips when Rex reached forward and grabbed Tania's hands.

"You getting this?" I whispered, leaning behind Jimmy to see what his phone was catching.

"Yeah," Jimmy shoved into me with his shoulder. "Don't blow our cover here."

Rex started kissing Tania's hands, slowly at first. His lips bulged over her lily-white skin, and as he continued, he increased his kissing speed and moved up her arm until finally stopping just below her elbow.

The dim-lit room couldn't hide the color of Tania's reddening cheeks.

"Let's get out of here, shall we?" Rex said loud enough for us to hear, pulling Tania out of her chair.

"Wait," I said, placing my hand on Jimmy's knee. "We can't let them see us."

"I'll pretend I'm going to the bathroom." Jimmy shot up off his stool and stormed towards the bathroom. I was sure he would blow our cover.

"Rex!" I shouted before Rex could spot Jimmy. "Fancy seeing you here!" I got up from my stool and walked towards the cash register. "We thought that was you, sitting across from us, but couldn't be sure."

"Marty!" Rex extended his big, veiny hand. I shook it.

"Hey Rex," Jimmy said, turning back from the bathroom and quickly slipping his phone into his pocket.

Rex shook Jimmy's hand.

"We miss you at the office," I said, making no eye contact with Tania.

Rex looked down at his car keys dangling in his fingers. "Yeah, sometimes things just don't work out, you know?"

Tania was half-turned from us, pretending to watch an ice hockey game on the TV above the bar.

"And then sometimes they do." Rex pulled Tania into his chest.

"Oh, Rex," she said in a feathery voice.

"It's okay, honey. Everybody's going to find out soon enough."

"I don't think we've met." Jimmy extended his hand.

"Tania."

"Nice to meet you, Tania." Jimmy shook her red-marked lily-white hand.

"Tania Sizemore." Rex kissed the top of her head.

"You don't say," I managed.

"Oh, Rex." Tania put a finger over her lip. "Shhh," she whispered.

Rex turned to the lady behind the cash register, handing her his credit card.

"I don't care if you tell him, boys."

Just before walking across the threshold, Rex hugged and kissed Tania. "I'll see you later, baby. I'm going to chat with these boys for a second."

We watched Tania drive away in her sky-blue Lexus.

"I'd actually like it if you told him. I want him to know where his little Tania's keeping warm at night."

Rex smiled. "So how'd he end up breaking the news to you boys?"

Jimmy and I said nothing.

"Well, c'mon, the number one salesman just gets canned out of the blue. And no explanation?"

"He said you were too cocky," Jimmy answered.

Rex laughed. "I guess that's one way to put it. Don't matter, though. You know what, boys?" He paused.

"What?" I asked.

"Your old pal, Rex, will be just okay."

Rex was tall and trim. He had a perfectly square jaw-line and thick silky black hair, movie-star-like.

"How'd you mean?" I noticed Jimmy reaching for his phone in his pocket.

I took a few steps back.

"I'll just leave it at that."

Rex couldn't help himself. "I'll put it this way for you, fellas. Lately, I've come to realize that I'm so much more than a life insurance salesman."

Jimmy glanced down at his phone and thumbed to his voice memo app. I watched him press the record button and then raise his phone awkwardly to his belly.

"So, Mrs. Sizemore?" Jimmy broke eye contact. "No offense, Rex. She's not exactly what I'd call your type."

Rex smiled, combing a hand through his hair. "I'm not sure whether to take that as a compliment or an insult."

"How'd the two of you meet?" I said quickly. "You both seem to be very much in love."

Rex reached into his jeans pocket and pulled out a carton of Marlboro Red. "I'm just messing, boys. I know what you mean. She's not the prettiest gal in the parlor. Or the smartest. But I'm telling you, we got something good going. Something real good."

*

Jimmy and I spent a week collecting photos, videos, and voice memo recordings. We even followed them to a park one evening, watching them make out like high-schoolers in Rex's pickup truck.

Mr. Sizemore called us into his office each morning that week, closing the door gently, then sitting us down, wide-eyed and hungry for information.

"We need a few more days," I said on our seventh meeting. "We almost have it all."

Eager as Jimmy was to show Mr. Sizemore what we'd documented, I convinced him to keep it close to our chests until the time was right.

"I'll give you two more days." Mr. Sizemore slammed his hand on his desk.

There was a brief silence.

"And how exactly will we be rewarded for our work?" I asked, pressing my sweaty palms into the desk.

"Excuse me?" He leaned in closer, arms stretched, palms flat.

"We've neglected some of our most important accounts this week, Mr. Sizemore."

Sizemore's eyes bulged. His top lip on the right side quivered like a puppeteer was moving it with a string.

I thought he was about to hit me, but his phone began vibrating. Sizemore straightened, grabbing his phone. On the screen, I read the name of the incoming call.

Sizemore flipped the phone over on its face.

"You'll be compensated for your extra work. Please, don't worry about that." His tone turned apologetic and measured.

I took a deep breath. "Could we get that in writing, Mr. Sizemore?"

Bracing myself, I was surprised when Sizemore turned towards his computer. He opened a Word document, then typed without saying anything. After printing the document, he signed two copies, handing one each to me and Jimmy.

The last line of the four-line document read, "Once all the evidence is received, you'll be given five thousand dollars."

Jimmy grabbed a pen from his shirt pocket.

I thrust my arm over his chest.

"Make it ten thousand, and we've got a deal."

My heart beat the speed of a hunted animal. Jimmy put his pen back into his pocket. I slid the contracts back to Sizemore. His eyes looked like boning knives. Taking what felt like a 40-second breath through his nose, then exhaling, Sizemore turned back to his computer. "Very well," he finally said. "You're life-insurance salesmen, after all, aren't you?"

We chuckled awkwardly. Sizemore printed a new contract. We signed it without speaking another word.

Walking us to the door, Sizemore shook our hands before we exited his office. "Two more days, gentleman."

It took every bit of restraint from Jimmy and I to say nothing to each other for the rest of the workday, to share not so much as a glance.

"Meet you at the Pocket?" I said to Jimmy after clocking out.

*

The place was empty. There was no sign of Rex and Tania.

"Afternoon, gentleman. Nice seeing you back so soon." A leathery-faced waitress forced a smile.

"We're going to take that table in the back," I said, walking past her.

I scanned the room again as we sat down. "There's a hell of a lot more going on here, Jimmy."

"What do you mean?"

"You saw that call, right?"

"No, who was it from?"

"It was Rex!"

"It was!?"

The waitress walked towards us. "Two Heinekens," I shouted before she got to our table.

"Did you see how his entire demeanor changed?"

"I did. What the hell's going on here?"

We sipped on our beers, not talking much. I held my hand, signaling for the waitress to bring another two beers when we were close to finishing.

"Pass me your phone, would you?" I said.

"Why?"

"I just want to review all we've got."

Jimmy patted his pockets, then stood up, searching under the table and seat. "Damn, I think I left it back at the office."

"I'll drive back with you. There's something we're missing, Jim. I just know it."

When I pulled into the parking lot, I noticed Sizemore's black Cadillac in its usual space. I waited for Jimmy outside the entrance to our building. As he parked, I spotted a red pickup truck across the street.

"Jim," I whispered.

Jimmy stopped near his car and looked around. "What is it?"

"Doesn't Rex drive a truck like that?"

Sprinting across the street, Jimmy peered into the truck's tinted windows.

"I'm pretty sure that belongs to Rex."

"Well, Jim, I don't know our play here."

"Me too." He said, panting.

"If Sizemore's office door's closed, we'll sneak in quietly and try to hear as much as possible."

Jimmy nodded.

"If it's open, we'll figure it out as we go."

He nodded again.

As soon as we reached the top of the stairs, we heard a scream from Rex. "I won't be Mr. Butterfly Man for another two more months! You said a couple of weeks! Max!"

Sizemore's door was open. I grabbed Jimmy's wrist and motioned to the printer with my eyes. Crouching behind the printer, we listened.

"You know much money's on the line here, Rex! Do you!? You won't have to work another day in your life!"

"What more do you need!? Rufus and Dufus have all the evidence, right? I couldn't have made it any easier for them."

"It's not that," Sizemore said. "I looked at the prenup again. I'll get half of everything if we reach twenty years. That's got to be at least $10 million now that her daddy's dead."

Jimmy lost his balance, grabbing the printer to steady himself. He hit a button, and paper spewed out of the tray.

"What's that?" Sizemore said, alarmed.

I pulled Jimmy around the table, positioning us behind the water fountain.

We heard their footsteps, then a pause.

"It's just the printer," Rex said, picking up the paper on the floor.

"It'll be twenty years in two months. I'll give you an extra two hundred thousand." Sizemore urged.

They stepped back into Sizemore's office.

"Five hundred. Not a penny less."

"You're a greedy son of a bitch, Rex. I could've got just about anyone for her to fall in love with."

"Trust me, there's only one Mr. Butterfly Man. Just ask Tania."

There was a jingling sound of keys, then footsteps. "Have it your way, Sizemore. I'll break the news to little Tania tonight." Rex said.

"Fine. Five hundred, but only after I get what's mine. You hear?"

I nudged Jimmy's shoulder, pointing to the door. We tiptoed out of the office and sprinted down the stairs into the parking lot.

"I didn't get my phone," Jimmy said, panicked.

"We don't need it. We're going to visit Tania Sizemore."

*

When we pulled into the subdivision, I scanned the houses on the left, and Jimmy the ones on the right. We spotted Tania's blue Lexus parked outside a home at the end of a cul-de-sac.

Tania opened the door before we had a chance to ring the bell. "You're the guys from The Corner Pocket."

"Good afternoon, Mrs. Sizemore. May we come in? We have something very urgent to tell you."

Tania's eyes widened. "What is it?"

"Nobody's hurt. We just need five minutes of your time." I said.

Tania led us into an expansive living room decorated with an African-themed motif. Jimmy and I sat on a zebra-skinned sofa, while Tania pulled up a tortoise-shelled bar stool.

"I'll cut right to the chase, Mrs. Sizemore. Your husband hired Rex to have an affair with you."

I leaned back into the sofa, half expecting Tania to fall forward off the stool. Instead, she smiled and began chuckling. "Oh really? And why in the world would he do that?"

"So he can take half of what you've got," Jimmy interjected.

"Your twentieth anniversary is coming up in two months, right?"

Tania nodded. "And so?"

"If he has proof that you're cheating on him, he'll take half of everything."

Getting up off the stool, Tania walked towards the liquor cabinet and poured a shot of vodka. "Rex is in love with me. There's nothing you can say to convince me otherwise." She downed the shot, then poured another.

"He hired us to get the evidence. Your husband. He's going to take half the inheritance you got from your father; then he's going to pay Rex. We have it all documented." I said.

Setting the shot glass to her lips, Tania took a small sip. "We're moving in together, you know? At the end of this month."

I stood up. "Mrs. Sizemore, you have to believe us. We're here to save you a lot of money and heartache."

She downed the rest of the vodka.

"And what's in it for you?"

"Two hundred grand. A hundred each." I said.

"We'll give you the evidence we've gathered. We haven't given anything to your husband." Jimmy paused. "Yet."

Tania slammed the shot glass into the bar stool. "You're crooks!"

She shoved her finger into Jimmy's chest, then mine. "You're trying to rip me and Rex apart. We're in love! Get the hell out of here, or I'll call the police!"

"Mrs. Sizemore, please."

"I'm counting to ten. One."

I grabbed a business card from my wallet. "If you change your mind, please call me immediately."

"Two!"

I dropped my card onto the floor. Jimmy and I scrambled out before she got to ten.

"Meet you at the Pocket," I said to Jimmy.

We grabbed two beers from the barman and found a table in the back.

I took a big sip. "Let's give the evidence to Sizemore on Monday and get out of this with our ten grand."

"You really think so? Now that we've told her everything. I'm afraid this comes back to bite us in the ass." Jimmy gulped.

"We've done nothing wrong." I said.

"I don't know, Marty. You think it's worth it?"

"Damn straight it is! We ain't leaving this mess without something."

We drove to the office after our beers. Sizemore and Rex had already left. After scanning the evidence on Jimmy's phone, I convinced Jimmy that we'd hand it over to Sizemore after the weekend.

*

Jimmy met me in the parking lot on Monday, twenty minutes before our usual clock-in time. "Any word from Tania?" He whispered as we walked up the stairs.

"Nothing."

I knocked on Sizemore's door.

"Come in," he said in a low, cracked voice.

His head was in his hands.

"We've got it all here for you, Sir." Jimmy set his phone on Sizemore's desk.

Sizemore didn't say anything, not looking at us.

"Everything okay, Mr. Sizemore?" I asked.

Picking up a manila folder, he poured its contents onto his desk. "You know what this is?"

We shook our heads.

"Divorce papers. From her attorney."

Jimmy and I looked at each other with raised eyebrows.

"She's in love with Mr. Butterfly Man, and apparently, he's in love with her too. We've been played, boys."

"Mr. Butterfly Man?"

Sizemore looked up. His eyes were narrow on his flushed, tomato-red face. "Rex! You damn idiots!"

"But what about the prenup?" I said, not caring now if he knew what we knew.

Sizemore sifted through the papers on his desk. He picked one up and faced it toward Jimmy and me. "Says right here she's got evidence that I hired Rex to have an affair with her. That damn crook. I should've known it."

Jimmy's neck shortened, like a tortoise pulling back into his shell. "Do we still get a little something, boss? I've got all the evidence right here." Jimmy picked up his phone off the table.

Sizemore slapped Jimmy's hand. The phone fell to the floor. "Get the hell out of here! The both of you!"

We clocked out early that day, right after Sizemore left.

"Want to get a beer at the Pocket?" I said as we walked across the parking lot.

"Might as well."

We sat down at a table in the back. Before taking a sip from our beers, we saw Rex walk in with an older-looking red-haired lady.

"Good evening, gentleman." Rex stopped at our table. "I'd like you both to meet, Mandy."

Mandy smiled, tilting her head as though a little embarrassed. I stared at the beautiful diamond-studded crucifix around her neck.

"Nice to meet you, Mandy," Jimmy said, extending his hand.

"We're on a date," Rex winked.

Mandy blushed.

"Isn't that right, little darling?"

Mandy's eyes sparkled as she looked up at Rex. "Yes, I think we are, Mr. Butterfly Man."

A Fool's Inheritance

The dimly lit, red-brick joint displayed black and white framed photos of opera singers, men in hats smoking cigars, and fresh produce spread out on wooden cutting boards.

"Complimentary bread?" Our waitress gestured, looking very Italian herself, olive-skinned, her dress's neckline covering her chest, as she stood at least two inches taller in her sleek, black stilettos.

"With extra basil," Janice, my mother-in-law, requested.

I pulled out my phone as soon as our waitress turned for the kitchen. I opened the showing for the home Mary and I loved. I moved the vase holding a red rose, setting my phone on the table, so my in-laws could see the listing. "We think this is the one right here. No doubts about it."

Mary glanced at me with her don't-put-your-foot-in-your-mouth expression.

"Oh, not this one! I'm not fond of the detached living area at all!"

"I am," I mumbled.

Mary kicked my shin.

"And there's no space for a garden!"

"We'd like a small garden," Barry, my father-in-law, remarked softly, his eyes on Janice the entire time.

"This is the one we love." Janice set her phone next to mine, swiping her screen with giant finger strokes, scrolling through the images.

"I do like the garden," I said. "And the pool."

"Well, we'd probably replace…"

"Hush, Barry," Janice barked, slapping her husband on the wrist before he could finish his sentence. "It's a beautiful house; look at all the space!"

"I'm not sure about sharing a kitchen, though," I said.

Mary gently set her palm on my hand. "We'll just need to establish some boundaries, that's all. Right, Mom?"

The waitress returned with the bread and the extra basil.

"This isn't the proper kind," Janice mumbled as she pinched the basil in her fingertips. "The real Italian kind is much bigger and more of a medium dark green."

"Well, we better inform them right away! God forbid they give us the wrong basil!"

"Steven!" Mary slapped my hand.

"What?" I smiled, landing my eyes on Mary's cold stare. The young waitress stood with her hands behind her back, grinning awkwardly.

"I think we're ready to order," I said, attempting to disarm the mildly tense situation.

"Speak for yourself, Steven!" Janice growled.

The waitress set the menus back on the table. "How about I give you folks a few more minutes?"

"Yes, that would be good, thank you," Barry placed his palm over Janice's hand.

"If you don't want to share a home with us, just come out and tell us, Steven." Janice slid her hand from under Barry's grip.

"Now, come on. That's not it at all. I'm just looking for a little diplomacy here." I narrowed my eyes on Mary, hoping she'd say something, but she didn't.

I grabbed Janice's phone and scrolled through the photos of their desired house. "Well, how about we put a door at the top of the stairs? Just to give us a little feeling of our own space, you know? I do love this garden; very tropical and lush."

Janice frowned, then pressed her palms into the table as though she were about to stand up, "Well, damn it. You…"

"A door sounds perfectly fine, Steven." Barry began rubbing Janice's back. "A beautiful garden, I agree, very Shangri-La looking, isn't it?"

"You folks ready to order?" Our waitress returned with another basket of bread.

"Just give me the parmesan chicken. You do serve that, right?" Janice moved back in her seat, reclining with a look of loss.

"I guess I'll have that too," said Barry, his hand still moving back and forth on his wife's back.

"One of the most popular items on the menu!" the young waitress offered.

"Me too." I handed her my menu.

"And you, ma'am?"

Mary possessed such calm during any big decisions we'd have to make, but not for something minor and insignificant, like what to order at the local Italian joint; she'd turn into a nervous wreck.

"I bet you'll love the chicken, honey." I gently grabbed her menu, tugging it upward.

"Do you mind!?" She snapped, showing me something fierce in her eyes. She looked up at our waitress. "How's the risotto?"

"Best on the island."

"I bet you say that about every dish," I mumbled, unafraid of aiming my frustration at the young girl.

"You're in such a sour mood tonight, aren't you, Steven?" Janice moved the salt and pepper to lock her cold eyes on me.

I made two fists under the table, squeezed until I felt weak, and then I stood up and touched the waitress on the shoulder. "I'm sorry for my rude comment, ma'am."

She smiled and giggled nervously.

"Mind pointing me to the restroom?"

"Right over there by that Pavarotti photo."

I'd been practicing ten minutes of daily silence for over a month to deal with stress and anxiety. I sat on the toilet, my pants raised, and leaned forward with closed eyes, chin on my fists. The idea was to become a passive observer of everything entering and exiting one's mind. I felt the rage grip my body, a wave of anger mainly directed at Janice. I let it go, watching it as though observing a neighbor walking his dog. When I returned to our table, I looked at all of them and smiled.

"Feel better," Mary asked, clutching my hand gently.

"Much...I'm sorry for being a little difficult, everybody. It's just that it's a big decision."

Janice handed me her phone, swiping the screen with giant strokes again. "If you'll just look at this one again..."

I nudged my palm into her phone, gesturing for her to take it back. "It's okay. I've made my decision."

"You have?" They all said in unison.

I picked up Mary's hand and placed it between mine, moving my eyes to Barry and Janice. "I think this is the one."

"You do?" Janice exclaimed.

"Yes, if you and Barry agree to front the entire purchase. In that way, everybody gets what they want."

"What!?" Mary shouted, snatching her hand from my grasp.

"And then we'll get the top unit?" Janice asked.

"Sure, it'd be your house, Janice."

Janice and Barry looked at each other, whispering.

They stood up with their hands outstretched. "Deal!"

"Wait a minute, how can you guys even afford that?" Mary put her arm between us, blocking any chance of a handshake. "I thought you needed us to put at least twenty-five percent down?"

"Oh, don't you worry about that," Janice said, smirking.

"It's a perfect idea, my love. That bottom unit will be a little tight initially, but we'll grow into it. And for the price of being mortgage-free!" I smiled, but Mary didn't smile back.

"We could try it out for a year. If it doesn't work, we'll have enough saved to buy a place of our own."

"Or sell and buy another house and move in together," Barry added.

All three of us stared at Mary, waiting for her approval.

"I guess it'll be a nice way to save some money and give us time to find a place of our own as we're adjusting to the island."

"Or buy a bigger place together," Barry said again.

Just then, our conversation was briefly interrupted by the arrival of the chicken parmesan. The waitress held a strained grin as the hot plates piled across her arm, red lines marking the plates' circumference on her olive skin.

"The risotto will be right out, ma'am."

Barry, Janice, and I looked at each other as the steam from our hot plates hit our noses.

"It's okay, go ahead, you guys," Mary eventually offered.

"Are you sure?"

"Of course," Mary said, smiling.

When the waitress returned with the risotto, Mary whispered something into her ear. The young girl disappeared, quickly returning with a bottle of Dom Pérignon.

"A toast to our new home!" Mary shouted, passing the generous glasses of champagne to us as quickly as the waitress had finished pouring.

"So it's a yes?" Janice asked.

Clutching my hand, Mary looked at me, beaming. "Yes! Let's do it!"

*

The bottom unit was satisfactory; more spacious than the photos revealed. The only trouble was the lack of a door at the top of the stairs, separating us from the kitchen. Janice threw a fit when I came home one day with a door and a set of tools. "If you put a door up, Steven, you might as well find your own place!"

So I left it alone. As a result, Janice and Barry went up and down the stairs as they pleased, present during our Friday movie nights, spectating Mary's and my chess matches, and eating every dinner with us.

It was a week before Janice and Barry's departure for their Italian vacation when the idea came to me. Turning to Mary, hours before the morning light, I whispered, "I know what I'm going to do."

"About what?" she mumbled.

"Your mom and dad. The door."

"Just forget it already. Another year, and we'll have enough saved to buy our own place."

"I'm going to get James to give me an audit."

Mary rolled over, grabbing my shoulders. "What!?"

"He'll draw up something for me stating that we'll need to put up a door for our space to qualify as my home office. They'll have to understand that."

"James McDermot? I remember him being very nosy. What happens when he finds out we're cheating on our taxes by claiming that home office?"

155

"I won't tell him anything about who owns the house and who pays what."

Mary turned on her side, curling her body, but then quickly turned back to me, whispering. "If they ever find out, we'll never get that inheritance; you do realize that?"

*

James met me at the house a few hours after I'd dropped Janice and Barry at the airport. He was a childhood friend who happened to be living on the island, working for the IRS. I wasn't sure exactly what he did for the IRS.

I led James through the kitchen and down the stairs to our space. "So I normally do my work just right over here." I pointed to my laptop resting on a table.

"Right here on this sofa?" James asked with surprise.

"Yup, I don't want you to do anything that feels uncomfortable, of course. A simple citation on some official-looking document will do, stating we need a door. You feel okay with doing that?"

"That's easy," he said, smiling. "I got some tough in-laws myself."

James continued inspecting the area with attentive eyes. It seemed strange to me that he wanted to see so much of our space. "Well, thanks, James. I appreciate it, man." I began walking up the stairs; my neck craned towards him.

He followed slowly. "So, what kind of setup you got with the in-laws?"

"What do you mean?"

"I imagine you're paying them rent then if you're taking the downstairs unit."

"Yes, that's right," I replied, quickening my steps.

"And what are their names again?"

"Why?"

"Oh, just curious, Steve. Not sure I've met them."

"Janice and Barry," I replied quickly, looking down at him from the kitchen.

"Kroh?"

James was studying the family crest framed above the staircase.

"Yes. Thanks for coming, James. I appreciate this."

"Like the bird, except with a K and an H."

I pretended not to hear him. "So you'll have something for me before they get back? Just in case they don't take my word for it."

"Oh yeah, I'll email it to you tonight."

I finished putting the door up that afternoon. When I heard Mary's car pull into the driveway, I ran up the stairs.

"My God, you actually did it!"

"Yeah, I told you I was going to."

"They're not going to like this."

"James is emailing the document tonight."

"That easy, huh? Doesn't really fit the bill of a typical IRS agent."

"What do you mean?"

"Well, those guys are all by the book, aren't they?"

"Said he's got some tough in-laws too, more than happy to help a friend out." I smiled.

Mary frowned. She set her handbag on the counter. "Well, I just hope it doesn't backfire on us."

*

My hands were tense on the steering wheel during the drive home from the airport. Janice and Barry's eyes wore the tiredness of nearly a full day's travel. When I noticed Janice resting her head on Barry's shoulder, I turned the mirror, saying, "We got a bit of bad news while you were away."

Janice perked up, straightening her neck and leaning forward. "What's that? Nothing happened to the garden, did it?"

"No, the garden's fine."

"Well, then, what is it?" Janice's head was directly behind my elbow now.

"I had a surprise IRS visit. The officer said we'd need to erect a door from the kitchen leading down to our space to qualify the downstairs as my home office."

"Oh, that's not so bad." The worried expression in Barry's eyes waned.

Janice looked at him with contempt, then slapped his thigh. "Well, that's ridiculous. They're not allowed just to come in and do surprise visits. I'm going to report this."

The car swerved as the steering wheel slipped through my hands. "No, no, it's okay. I've already put the door up; it wasn't a big deal."

"I don't care about that! It's an invasion of privacy!"

There was a silence. Then, Barry spoke with a calculated tone. "It's actually very much in their jurisdiction, honey. And we definitely don't want to be putting our names in front of any IRS agent."

They looked at each other with a new anxiousness in their eyes. "Did he ask about us?" Barry questioned.

"No. Nothing about you."

Their faces seemed to soften. Janice returned to resting on Barry's shoulder. They said nothing further during the drive home.

*

Having the door made life in the house pleasant. I could now walk around in my underwear and have an honest conversation with Mary without the fear of being heard by her parents. We even got to eat a few dinners alone. Unfortunately, this lasted for just a little more than two weeks. One day, I returned from a jog to find Barry and Janice crying at the kitchen table, with papers in their hands.

"We're being audited!" Janice cried. "We're going to lose everything!"

"What?"

"Look!" Janice shoved the papers into my hand. I scanned the IRS citation and shuddered, reading the signature of the investigating officer. James McDermot.

"James," I muttered.

"What?"

"Does Mary know?"

"We're going to lose everything!"

I handed the document back to Janice. "Now, don't overact. It's not ideal, but how bad could it be? Just a little back taxes, no?"

"Did you read it? We've gone twenty years without paying taxes! Now they're coming for everything!"

"Twenty years!" My arms went stiff as boards. A chill ran down my spine. "How do you not pay taxes for twenty years?"

"Look, it's got to be the same guy that came over here when we were in Europe. Says we, we have an undocumented tenant in our house p-p-paying rent. Wh…wha what was that guy's name, Steven?" Barry's hands shook as he spoke, and his stutter that only appeared when he was nervous was as bad as I'd ever heard it.

"Was it James McDermott!?" Janice exclaimed.

"No, no. I'm not sure now." I opened the door and raced down the stairs. I kneeled behind the TV dresser with a blanket over my head, phone pressed to my ear.

"James, what have you done, man?!"

"Hi, Steve!"

"I need you to fix this."

"Oh, there's no fixing anything. Your in-laws have been playing outside the lines for a long time. One of my biggest catches to date! I thought you'd be pleased about this; get them off your case for good!"

"Please, James. You got to get them out of this."

"Too late for that now, I'm afraid."

*

We moved out of the house two weeks later. We used every dime Mary and I had saved for a down payment on a small two-bedroom condo fronting a public golf course.

Janice planted a basil garden right outside our bedroom window. She tends to it daily at dawn. All four of us eat breakfast, lunch, and dinner together. At night, I turn on a sound machine to help with the noise traveling through the paper-thin walls separating our bedrooms. The other evening at supper, Janice asked if I could get rid of it as it was disturbing her sleep.

"I've got a better idea," I said, smirking.

Mary grabbed my knee underneath the table and squeezed.

"Oh yeah, what's that?" Janice asked.

"Oh, nothing," I said, then stuffed a large red pepper into my mouth.

Love She Said

I walked into Brad's Ale House with a cigarette burning in my mouth and a five-dollar note in my pocket. I noticed an open seat between a Rabbi and a lady wearing a crucifix.

"What can I buy for you, my friend? Abel's the name." The Rabbi held out his hand, patting the ripped leather bar stool with the other.

"Jake," I said, shaking his hand. He looked at the woman for a second and then, when she met his gaze, he turned back to me. Abel had thick, dark eyebrows, bushy enough to comb each morning. A sharp hook-shaped nose extended over his dry lips, and he spoke with an accent.

"Canadian?" I asked.

He laughed, "I get that a lot." He pulled up the sleeve of his Kittel and showed me a purpled-tinged Prince tattoo.

The lady was still barely glancing at the Rabbi. The way her eyes and lips creased downward, her expression appeared scornful.

"Minnesota?" I smiled.

"You betcha!" He raised his shot glass, which I guessed was filled with whiskey, judging the amber color. He tossed it into his mouth like it was a splash of water.

As I sat down, the woman whispered. "Life ain't easy, handsome."

I nodded, grinning something anxious.

"Damn straight," Abel mean-mugged the woman, then refocused on me before saying, "So what you drinking, kid?" His eyes appeared more bloodshot.

"I'm not sure."

"Brad, get this man a double!"

Brad, the barman, was a short, stocky man with one of the most beautifully manicured handlebar mustaches I'd ever seen. He wore a yellowish stained cut-off white shirt and a train conductor's hat.

"On the rocks, stranger?"

"Sure."

"Looks like someone broke your heart, kid," Abel said.

I fiddled with a button on my baby blue cotton shirt.

"You know how I know?"

"How?" I mumbled.

"Your eyes. The eyes of a man don't lie." The way Abel's voice carried, it seemed he intended his words for the woman.

Brad set the double shot of whiskey in front of me. I slung it into my mouth, straining my face as the burn traveled down my back. Laughing, Abel shifted his gaze between me, Brad, and the lady. "That's how we all drink 'em, all of us broken-hearted types. Pour him another, Brad!"

I lifted my hand, politely refusing. Brad set the glass in front of me without hesitation, as though he'd been expecting Abel's instruction. I'd only eaten half a BLT at lunch, now more than six hours ago. I didn't finish it after Vicky told me she was leaving me.

"C'mon, kid, it's good for you; it helps with the pain." Abel nudged the glass towards me as a warm euphoria began roping my senses.

"What the hell," I mumbled, then threw the shot down as though I'd been drinking nightly doubles for twenty years.

"I only ever dreamed of two things," I looked down at the counter, tracing my finger into the names carved with a steak knife.

"And what's that?"

I craned my neck to view the woman. The late afternoon sun shone through a crease in the tinted window, brightening her silver crucifix. I turned back to Abel and then to the lady again before speaking, "A girl and a mission."

Abel nodded, puckering his lips. "Ain't that all of us, kid?" He raised his empty glass. "Be fruitful and multiply!"

"She said she'd leave me if I didn't stay. If I don't put my roots down in this godforsaken town."

"Well, do you love her?"

I traced my finger into a carving that read, Summer-of-85. "I think so."

Fiddling with the crucifix, the lady stood, driving her palms into the counter, looking at me with something fierce. "No, you don't."

"Now, now. Give the kid a break, will you?" Abel spoke sharply, standing and meeting the woman with a dirty look.

"Why'd you say that?" I asked the lady, feeling empowered.

She leaned towards me, her crucifix dangling in front of my eyes, her breath the scent of licorice. "Because any man who truly loves his woman will give up everything to have her." She momentarily made eye contact, then delivered Abel a death stare.

"Everything!?" Abel slammed his leathery hands onto the counter, turning his head to meet the woman's gaze.

"Everything!" the lady shouted, storming out of the bar.

"She'll be back tomorrow," Brad mumbled.

"I know," Abel replied, resting his head in his palms.

We sat in silence for a while. I felt unsure where to rest my eyes, eventually settling them on a TV showing a bull riding contest.

"We used to be in love." Abel's head turned slowly towards me. "Me and Terry." He pointed to the empty bar stool where the lady had been sitting.

"But then she found Jesus. And all of that changed." He snapped his fingers.

"And don't forget about Pastor Daniel," Brad added.

Abel nodded. "Yeah, he's part of it, for sure. She doesn't know how to wipe her own ass without getting clearance from that prick."

Abel began drumming his fingers on the counter, a slow, sad beat. "I used to be everything to her, and then just like that, I ain't nothing. Nothing more than a piece in her great divine puzzle. So you know what I did, kid?"

He slurred his words. I turned to look at him, and instead of being distracted by his thick eyebrows, I watched a stream of saliva trickle down his bottom lip. "What?" I managed.

"I became a damn Rabbi."

Brad chuckled and offered an expression that indicated he'd heard this story a hundred times.

"Why?"

Abel raised two fingers to Brad. "I don't know exactly why, kid. Maybe to show her, I could also find God."

"Did it work?"

"Not even a little. I pushed her further away. She told me we'd be done if I didn't get saved, whatever that means. That's why she's in here screaming about giving up everything for the one you love. That and she's so scared of going to hell, kid, scared that our love's going to send her there."

I looked at the Rabbi, half thinking about my situation with Vicky. "But you still love her?"

Abel stared into the counter, then turned to me with a longing in his eyes, "More than you know, kid."

Brad set two shot glasses of whiskey in front of Abel. Abel slid one of them over to me, then slammed the other down his throat. "But I ain't no puppet, kid, and neither are you!" His eyes were nearly completely red, and now, instead of looking like he was going to cry, he appeared rage-bent. "And that damn Pastor Daniel hasn't made things any easier—keeps telling her to stay away from me. He's why we divorced—kept telling her our marriage wasn't biblical! Whatever that means!" Abel let out big breaths as though struggling to breathe, or he was trying to calm himself; I couldn't tell. I noticed Brad studying Abel with a concerned expression, thumbing his mustache while wiping a clean glass. I stared at the shot of whiskey before me, trying to keep a steady gaze on Abel in my peripheral. Abel's head began bobbing back and forth, and his deep breathing became softer. He landed heavily on the counter within a few seconds, making a loud thud. Brad stepped closer and set a soft cushion under Abel's head, wiping the spit pooling between the old man's lips. "Happens at least once a week."

"That they run into each other?" I said, a little confused.

"Oh no, the fighting. And Abel drinking too much then passing out. They meet here every day." Brad had an eye on my shot glass. "Terry normally stays a lot longer, though."

"Why!?" I blurted out with surprise, curling my hands around my glass and pulling it closer to my chest.

"Because they love each other."

I poured the whiskey into my mouth and then let out a burning sound. "You're going to have to explain this all to me, Brad."

Brad took my glass, held it under a tap. He wiped it with the same rag he'd used earlier. "They started meeting here about two years ago after the divorce was finalized. Terry was a real zealot back then, way worse than she is now. She'd open and end their time together with prayer, wore long, loose dresses, virtually zero neckline."

I struggled to keep my eyes on Brad as I felt my head going light. His voice seemed to develop a trailing effect.

He put the glass down and moved closer. "Just saying she's eased up a little, that's all. The only reason why she lost it tonight is cause there's probably some revival happening at her church, and she's feeling guilty."

"So why don't they just get back together?"

Brad chuckled. "The human conscience is a powerful thing." He glanced at the Rabbi. "And so is religion. And Pastor Daniel, I guess. He's got some kind of grip on her. Wouldn't be surprised if he's trying to jump a ride on that pink canoe; take her behind the altar curtains, if you know what I mean?" Brad winked, then chuckled.

"But they still love each other?"

"Yeah. But like I said, when you think you're going to go to hell because you're married to a heathen, love doesn't really matter, does it?"

"The Bible says that?"

Brad poured a shot of whiskey into the glass I'd just drank from. "Apparently. At least according to Terry and Pastor Daniel. Hell, if I know, though, kid."

I stared into a neon-pink-lit mirror above the bottle rows of liquor, mulling it all over. The pink-lit frame seemed to swallow the mirror the longer I looked at it. Brad poured the shot into his mouth.

The same shade of pink as the mirror began cloaking Brad in my vision. "Well, why doesn't the Rabbi just become a Christian? Seems like that would solve everything."

Brad laughed, grabbing the bottle of whiskey again. "Abe's one of those old soul purists. It's what I love about him, a take-it-or-leave-it kinda guy, you know? He ain't about to jump on Terry's hamster wheel. He doesn't think that's the way love should work. Neither do I, frankly."

I stopped thinking about Abel and Terry, shifting my thoughts to Vicky.

Abel began snoring and moving his head. Brad immediately readjusted the pillow.

"It's not the same with me and Vicky, you know?"

Brad turned to me with confused but caring eyes.

"How does she expect me to stay in this town all my life? And do what? I want to see the world, you know? Make something of myself. Is that too much to ask?"

Stepping closer, the bottle of whiskey turning in his hand, it looked as though Brad was about to pour another shot. He started to speak when the saloon-style doors swung back and forth.

"Just a simple prayer and a water baptism. Is that too much to ask, Brad!?" Terry had been crying; her black mascara looked like lines a child had drawn down her cheeks.

"He doesn't think that's how love works, Terry, you know that." Brad tilted his head downward and kept his eyes on Abel as he spoke.

"I always thought the Bible spoke out against divorce. Didn't Jesus say something like that?" I said with a drunkard's confidence.

"Well, that's not what Pastor Daniel says! That's why I came back in here tonight." Terry stared at Abel, moving closer to him.

"What do you mean?" Brad set a shot of whiskey in front of Terry.

She slung it into her mouth, then slammed the shot glass on the counter. It made a sound like a Fourth of July drum.

"God Jesus, mother, Mary of Moses!" Abel almost fell off his bar stool, wobbling backward, reaching his hands towards Brad, who grabbed him by the fingers, securing him on the seat.

"He asked me to marry him."

The bottle of whiskey fell crashing to the floor, slipping out of Brad's hands.

"Pastor Daniel," Terry said.

"What?" Abel shouted, standing and approaching Terry with an untempered urgency.

"He says a woman needs a man, a God-fearing one. And he's right, you know. He's right, Abel!" Terry's voice was high and cracking now as she spoke. I kept looking for tears, but she succeeded in holding them back.

"Son of a god-damn bitch. He's been playing you all this time! Can't you see it?" Abel rolled up the sleeves on his Kittel, revealing trim, veiny forearms.

I began thinking about the old Sunday school lessons I'd learned as a kid. I was sure that the Bible and Jesus didn't condone divorce. Terry and Abel kept arguing while I grabbed my phone and began a Google search. After refining the search a few times, I found a great article titled "What Jesus and the Bible Say About Divorce."

When I looked up from my phone, Abel had his arms around Terry, and her head was in his chest, both crying.

"Read this!" I shouted, holding my phone up to them.

Abel grabbed my phone while Terry lifted herself off his chest. He set the phone on the counter, and they began reading the article.

"Well, I'll be damned," Abel dropped a gentle fist on his bar stool, and a broad smile appeared over his lips.

"How do we know it's true, though?"

"It's the Bible, Terry!"

The expression on Terry's face was not the same excited look that Abel possessed. She appeared nervous, as though about to be caught in a devious act. "So Pastor Daniel's been lying to me? You know how many times he said that a Christian woman couldn't be married to a heathen without the certainty of hell?"

Brad came up from the floor with a dustpan full of shattered glass. "Because he wants to butter your biscuit! That's why I don't go to church; too many bad players in the game." Brad reached for another bottle of whiskey, poured four shots, and passed them around.

Abel took Terry's hand, lifted her, and put her on his lap. He whispered something in her ear. She laughed nervously, then he raised his shot glass, saying with great triumph, "To the words of Jesus on marriage!"

Terry's face softened. She leaned into Abel's chest, clinking her glass to Abel's. Brad and I joined. "Cheers," we said in unison, pouring the whiskey into our mouths.

Abel squeezed my shoulder and rocked me back and forth. "Maybe we'll have another wedding! You got to be in it, kid!"

Terry smiled sheepishly, appearing as though still trying to make sense of it all.

"And you should bring your lady friend!" Abel added.

Abel touched my neck, gently massaging it with his thumb. "What are you thinking about her?"

Abel was a blurred blob of black in my vision as I turned to look at him.

"I guess I'm not sure now."

On the dim TV, I could make out an interview with a man who'd sailed around the world in a hundred and fifty-two days. I grabbed the remote and turned up the volume. He had his arm around a crying woman. The reporter moved towards the woman. "How did you do it? How were you able to let him go for that long?"

"Love," she said.

Janky Jenny

I read the job description with a smile, nursing my Miller Light.

Responsible for providing proficient written content using effective note-taking while exercising privacy and discreteness.

Got to be a government post, I thought. I reread the description and emailed the hiring company my resume, detailing my over forty years of administrative writing experience across the corporate and private sectors. The following day, I woke to the vibrating noise of my phone pounding into my drunk-sick temple.

"What is it?" I mumbled, sliding my finger across the screen.

"Mr. Jennings?"

I didn't recognize the man, but he spoke with pace and a sharp nervousness.

"I'd like to talk to Mr. Jennings, please."

I flung the curtain open, observing the death-black sky. "Who's calling at this godforsaken hour?"

"The name's Caneer, James Caneer. I'm the director of SBCL."

"SB, who?"

"The Men's and Women's Society for Business and Community Leadership."

"Never heard of it." I rolled out of bed, popping the lid from a bottle of ibuprofen.

"Well, I received your resume and I like the look of it. Would you be able to come in for an interview later to-day?"

I glanced at the empty cans of Miller Light on my bedrest. "Yes," I replied. "That was me. But I'm not so sure now to tell the truth. I've recently retired."

"What do you mean?" Caneer's voice cut a little sharper.

"Well, have you nobody else for the job?"

"I'll give you a twenty-thousand-dollar sign-on bonus. What do you say?"

I picked up a half-empty can, shook it gently, then finished it off. "Sure, what the hell."

"What was that?" He exclaimed. "You'll take it?"

I met Caneer at The Majestic, an expensive down-town hotel. The concierge led me to the ballroom, a chandelier-lit space with peach blossom wallpaper. A bottle of Dom Pérignon on ice rested in the middle of the long teak table.

Caneer was wearing a bowler hat and a black crease-less suit.

"You must be Mark Jennings?" He reached out his hand, removing his hat.

I stood up slowly but struggled to keep my eyes off his chin, which was short and dented like somebody had blasted a baseball bat into it.

"That's right. Mr. Caneer, I presume?"

"Call me James, please." His hand was cold and sweaty, and when I looked him in the eyes, he quickly moved his gaze to something behind me, then pulled his palm away and sat down.

"I run an important, small, but powerful collective."

I nodded.

"There are ten of us, all prominent businessmen and women, leaders in our various communities nationwide. We look for opportunities to better our towns and cities." Caneer paused, handing me a pamphlet. "I won't bore you with any more details; this provides a nice summary of our organization."

I flipped through the pamphlet, noticing more than a few grammatical errors.

"We need a writer, Jennings. A good one. I've been wanting to not only document our activities but also our profiles."

"Profiles?"

"Our stories, the lives of the men and women who make up the group: a fascinating lot who have something to say regarding how they've lived their lives."

I looked up and noticed his fingers drumming against the table. "Biographies?"

"Sure, I guess you could call it that."

I stared blankly at the wall behind him.

Standing with a puffed chest and hand outstretched, Caneer announced, as though he were talking over a noisy audience, "A hundred dollars an hour! Plus that twenty thousand dollar signing bonus, of course!"

I pretended to think about it for a while, then stood and shook his cold, wet hand for the second time. "When do I start?"

"How about today?"

I had my eyes on the Dom Pérignon as he said this.

"Oh, I'm sorry, I almost forgot!" He reached into his pocket for a bottle opener and uncorked the champagne.

"Today's fine," I said.

He didn't pour himself a glass and only filled mine halfway. When he set the bottle on the ice, I picked it back up and poured until my glass was full. I noticed his bushy brows forming a frown. I reached for his glass and filled it beside mine, sliding it toward him.

"I don't drink," Caneer said.

"What a shame," I said, reaching for his glass.

"We'll need to get you a driver, Jennings!"

I gulped the champagne like it was a morning cup of water. "Driver?"

"To get to the office, of course."

"I assumed you were operating out of one of these hotel rooms?"

I curled my hand around the second glass of champagne as Mr. Caneer moved the canister containing the bottle closer to his side of the table.

"Oh, of course not! Discreetness, remember, and the highest level of privacy. We don't want just anyone to know our whereabouts, Mr. Jennings. I couldn't be certain you would be our man. That's why I had you meet me here."

I sipped on the second glass, nodding, trying to keep my expression from appearing too curious.

"I'll call you a taxi."

"Don't do that; this has hardly ticked my spine." I raised my glass towards him. "I'll follow you."

I stayed with Caneer through the busy city traffic, finally turning left onto a narrow one-way street in a part of town where graffiti-sprayed buildings outnumbered the streetlights. We stopped in front of a dilapidated structure. Caneer's driver exited the black Lexus, scanned the area, and heaved the faded, rusty garage door open. Observing the derelict surroundings, I half thought I was about to get robbed, played into the hands of some scam on retirees. Nevertheless, I followed the Lexus into the building. The white-walled garage was empty, with enough space for at least ten cars.

Caneer led me through a fluorescent-lit hall, then stopped before a faded lime green door, fiddling with his keys. "You look surprised, Jennings?"

"A little, If I'm honest."

When he opened the door, I noticed a petite, blonde-haired girl with rose-blush skin sitting at a desk. I couldn't see the color of her eyes because she was staring down at her phone. "Jenny, my girl, you're early." Caneer reached for Jenny's hand and squeezed it gently, curling his other arm around her back.

"Jennings, this is my dear daughter, Jenny, on track for a scholarship to Brown or Harvard!"

Jenny didn't look up from her phone.

"Please, Jenny, say hello to my friend."

She lifted her head for half a second and smiled.

"It's true, she's going to get into one of those schools with a full ride, Jennings! Mark my words!" The vigor Caneer spoke with seemed forced. Jenny didn't appear to hear a single word, her eyes glued to her phone, laughing at every third swipe of her finger.

"Follow me, Jennings."

We walked into a corner room no bigger than a utility closet. Caneer removed his bowler hat, revealing his balding scalp, then closed the door, making the room feel smaller. "Flying under the radar is how I like to put it, Jennings. Why rent out the Majestic and announce one's intentions to the world?"

I tried my best not to look at the combed tufts of hair on either side of his reddish chicken-skin scalp. I started getting flashbacks of old illustrations I'd seen as a kid in church, of Moses parting the Red Sea.

"Well? Jennings?"

"Well, what?" I said, moving my eyes to Caneer's deformed chin.

"Inconspicuousness. A noun. Oh God, please tell me you get it?"

I didn't care about making an impression on Caneer, but I was curious. I cleared my throat. "Makes perfect sense. Hidden from public scrutiny, a clandestine organization that operates…" I held my palms to the ceiling and scanned the room, as though absorbing the space into my hands and eyes. "In the shadows!"

Caneer clapped. "Yes! Quite observant! You do get it!"

I strained a smile until he opened a rusty, banged-up filing cabinet. "It's in here somewhere, Jennings; just give me a minute, would you."

I was examining the wrinkles on the back of my hand when he shoved the file underneath my nose.

"You're going to need this."

The paper file was faded red, sheets exploding out the sides.

"All the details of nine people's lives. Right in here, Jennings. In abbreviated form, of course, outlines, as you writers say. I'll need your expertise to expand the bullet points here. Craft something compelling, something that feels real."

"Real? And only nine? I thought there were ten of you?"

"Well, um, yes, my profile isn't included." Caneer began drumming his fingers against the table.

"Nine believable biographies, Jennings."

"Believable?" I turned over the page, reading the first name, Larry McDeed. Caneer slammed his big hand onto the file. "It's all here, Jennings. Everything you need." He moved even closer. Above the folder, I caught a blurry glimpse of his red belt buckle. "We're talking about high-level shit here."

Caneer removed his hand. I glanced at the childlike scribbles of the notes in the folder. "Are these your notes?" I said, looking up at him.

Snatching the folder, Caneer began thumbing through the pages. "Yes, what's wrong? There's nothing wrong here, is there?"

I placed my fingers gently on the folder, then tugged. He let it go. "Should I start today?"

He stared with a knotted expression. "Well, yes. Start today. You can use this room. Don't hesitate to ask me any questions, okay, Jennings?" Caneer squeezed out from behind the desk.

I nodded, turned the folder right side up, and opened to the first page to read the notes on Larry McDeed.

"Let me go get you a chair. And the laptop. Yes, you'll need that laptop, of course, Jennings."

When Caneer returned, I'd finished skimming through his notes on McDeed. "Quite the entrepreneur this Mr. McDeed is, isn't he?"

Dropping the chair with the back of it facing the table, Caneer rushed over to me. "Did you go through all of it? The part about the whores? Look, it's all here." He pointed to a scribble of words near the bottom of the page. His voice was frazzled and high-pitched.

"Yes, I noticed that. A busy man!" I offered a big smile and a chuckle, but this seemed to undo Caneer further.

"It's most important to expound upon every detail accurately and precisely, leaving nothing out! Pay special attention to highlighting the…" he paused, searching.

I thumbed through the folder aimlessly, then looked up. "The incriminating parts?"

A kind of relief washed over his face.

"Well, sure, I wouldn't quite put it like that, but okay, you get where I'm going. Trust me, it's all for a good purpose, I promise you."

"When do you need it by?"

Caneer raised his finger, "Just a minute, Jennings." He rushed out of the room, calling for Jenny.

He returned within minutes, his face flushed and a bead of sweat dripping down his long forehead. "By the end of the week, Jennings. Just in time for the board meeting."

"I'll have to take this home with me then," I said, craning my neck and examining the folder.

"Absolutely not!" Caneer slammed his hand against the table. "This is far too classified for anything of the sort, Jennings!"

I didn't say anything, staring blankly, making sure Caneer couldn't detect even a wrinkle of bother on my face.

"You can take this key. Come and go as you please."

I took the key and slid it into my pocket.

"Jenny and I are heading out now. That key will lock up everything."

I was about to ask him about the twenty-thousand-dollar sign-on bonus, but then I got distracted by a small fridge at my feet.

"I'll have it ready for you by the end of the week, not sparing a single detail."

Caneer sighed. A broad smile overtook his chubby face. "Excellent, I knew you were the man for the job!"

I found a six-pack of Busch Light in the fridge. I threw three into the small freezer section, and opened the red folder again.

It didn't take long to notice the same pattern in each biography.

Susan Harris, married with three kids; chief investment banker of United Trust; cheating on her husband with a high school quarterback.

Paul Rose; single; the nation's leading ear specialist; struggling with a cocaine addiction.

I turned to the last page of the folder to a James Tims, CEO of SmartGames; married with four young kids to a super-model wife; owing the IRS over a million dollars.

A small asterisk at the bottom left corner of the page caught my attention. I would've missed it if not for Caneer's paragraph reiterating the simple instructions for the job. Beside the asterisk, written in the same child-like handwriting, was the word *Harvard.*

I flipped through the folder again, starting with Larry McDeed. Sure enough, the same asterisk was at the bottom of each biography with either *Harvard* or *Brown* penned next to it. I finished the project that night, dressing Caneer's shorthand with a touch of calculated eloquence and extra details I thought Caneer would find helpful, if not amusing. As a case in point, I made Mr. Larry McDeed not only guilty of acting out his schoolboy lust but also a whore-man himself, pushing girls to friends for favors. McDeed's Dirty Deeds, I called the operation, and continued similarly for every man and woman in the red folder.

My curiosity dragged me out of bed the following morning back to Caneer's inner-city dump of an office. Jenny was sitting in the same seat as when I'd first met her, zombie-like, scrolling on her phone. "Good morning, Jenny," I said, tilting my head downward to catch her eyes. She didn't look up. I stepped closer, wondering when and if she might notice me. She didn't. I moved even closer. She was engulfed in cat videos and then a series of videos of clowns holding purple umbrellas. Even when I joined her in forced laughter at some half-ass comical act on the screen, she remained oblivious to my presence.

"Jennings! Just the man I wanted to see today!"

I followed Caneer into the small room. "Harvard or Columbia, you say?"

Caneer froze, his back turned to me. His hands curled into fists at his sides, and his shoulders raised as though he were inhaling a great weight of air. "I'm paying you a lot of money, Jennings!" He didn't turn to look at me. "You don't need to worry about anything other than doing your damn job!"

I backed up. "Well, of course, Mr. Caneer. My sister went to Harvard. I was merely curious which school Jenny preferred."

Caneer's body instantly went limp as he let out a sigh, turning around with a giant smile. "Oh, you're talking about my Jenny?"

Exaggerating a confused frown, I stepped closer. "Well, what else did you think I was talking about?"

"Oh, nothing, my mistake, Jennings. I'm sorry you caught me at a bad time here. The board meeting is today! I got my dates sideways! I'll need you to have the biographies ready by noon."

I forced my tongue between my teeth, then strained my cheeks like I'd tasted something sour. When I saw Caneer's hands turn into tight fists again, I said, "Not a problem, Mr. Caneer."

His hands relaxed.

"But I'd think it'd be best if I were present at that meeting."

Caneer's body became one giant hot air balloon.

"And what in God's green earth makes you say that, Jennings?" He stepped closer, standing on his tiptoes.

I removed a notepad from my backpack and lifted it in front of his eyes. "It's just notes, more like scribbles only I can decipher. Alternatively, I could try to crank out a shortened version of each biography and possibly have it ready by noon. I may have to leave out a few details, though."

Caneer squinted, then clutched the notepad out of my hands. "Looks like chicken scratch."

"I'll start working on the abbreviated version," I said, quickly reaching for the notepad.

"Now, just wait, give me a minute to think about this, will you." Caneer threw the notepad on the table. And then, after a brief moment, he picked it up again and studied it with strained eyes. "You sure you'll be able to decipher this? Without leaving out any details?"

"I'm certain," I replied.

Handing the notepad back to me, Caneer clapped his hands together. "Right, this is what we're going to do."

He locked the door, then proceeded with a much softer voice. "I'm going to conduct the board meeting while you wait outside. I'll then collect you, and you'll present each biography to the board, sparing no detail. No questions asked. Do you understand?"

I nodded.

Opening the drawer in the small table, Caneer pulled out a razor. He handed it to me with three hundred dollar notes. "Shave, then go buy something suitable to wear, please. I can't have you looking like Don the Beachcomber." I glanced at my Aloha shirt and paint-stained khakis, then moved my palm over my sandpaper chin. "Certainly," I said, not knowing whether to smile or furrow my brow.

When I returned a few hours later, the foyer was a hive of business suits. Standing in the corner, I began playing a game with myself, seeing if I could match the faces to the biographies I'd written. I was honing in on a chat between a tall, greasy-haired man and a curvy woman wearing a red skirt. Straightening my black tie and readjusting my shirt collar, I walked up to the man, reached out my hand, and said, "You must be Larry." Then I turned to the woman, "And Susan, I presume?" They both looked at me as though I were holding a dead bird. Before either could respond, Caneer came out of the closet room, shouting, "Alright, let's get this meeting started with, Ladies and Gentlemen."

Everybody filed into the room, Caneer holding the door like a butler. Once they were all in, he closed the door and approached me with a tight, anxious face. "What did you say to them? Who've you been speaking to?"

"Nothing. Nobody." I adjusted my tie. "Do you like my outfit?"

"You just be ready, Jennings." Caneer barked.

About ten minutes later, he came out of the closet room with a brow dripping sweat. "You ready? Just like we spoke about, you hear?"

I nodded.

Caneer directed me to a small corner of the room. I hadn't noticed the Egyptian-themed wallpaper before. I was getting lost in the hieroglyphics, pyramids, and pharaohs when Caneer snapped, "Alright, Jennings, go ahead with your presentation, please!"

I pulled out my notepad from the sweaty pocket of my new blazer, holding it out in front of me as though it were the very papyrus of Tutankhamen himself.

"Now remember, no interruptions, please!" Caneer had moved his chair to face the men and women sitting around the table, his back to me.

Without looking any of the suits in the eyes, I read through their scandalous biographies, sparing no juicy details.

Midway through McDeed's biography, Larry stood up, laughing, "What the hell is this?" Caneer didn't say a word, his reaction a little more than a blink of his eyes. I tried not to smile. After finishing McDeed's biography, Caneer stood, "Now remember, as we've already discussed, these go live at the press of a button." Caneer showed his phone to the group, landing his gaze on Larry McDeed. "So, for your own good, exercise some damn restraint!" He looked at me with pulsing eyes, "Carry on, Jennings!"

When I finished reading the last biography, there was a surprising silence in the room, the suits all staring at each other. Susan Harris finally said, "Such good writing; one could easily believe it for truth."

"Exactly!" Caneer shouted.

"You telling me you go to all this trouble for a few lousy recommendation letters?"

McDeed turned to me. "I hope he's paying you in diamonds."

"That'll be all, Jennings, thank you."

I didn't move, intrigued by the unfolding situation.

"Thank you, Jennings." Caneer barked again.

"Let the man stay, Eric!" James Tims exclaimed. "He's as deep in the shit as you are now."

"Yes! He stays!" a few others shouted in unison.

I sat down, avoiding eye contact with Caneer. He said nothing, squaring his shoulders to the suits around the table.

Mr. Brady coughed, then announced, "Sure, I'll write Janky Jenny a recommendation letter to Harvard. That's no skin off my back. Just don't publish that shit about me, please. There's no scrubbing that in today's world."

A few of the suits began nodding, Caneer grinning with every movement of their heads.

"Well, I certainly won't!" Mrs. Harris slammed her palms onto the table. It's the principle. And well, the obvious."

"The obvious?" Canneer asked with a massive V-shaped frown.

Mrs. Harris scanned the room. Nobody made eye contact; everybody looked down.

"Well, Janky Jenny, of course." Mrs. Harris finally offered. "She won't make it a day in a university of any kind, Eric. You've got to see that. Surely?"

Canneer didn't flinch, searching the room with an empty expression.

It was a few seconds of awkward silence before Paul Rose stood and started towards the door. "Go ahead, press publish. See if I care. You can't believe anything on the internet these days. I'm not writing a recommendation letter for Janky Jenny."

"I'll write two letters for Janky Jenny; just don't press publish, please, Eric." Mr. Brady blurted.

Paul Rose was standing at the door with his palm on the handle and a surprised expression on his face. "You're telling me they're going to give Janky Jenny a high school diploma?"

Something began to change on Caneer's face. His cheeks began to crease. His eyes thinned.

"Damn good question, Paul!" Susan exclaimed, "No way Janky Jenny makes it out of high school!"

Caneer's chair screeched against the tiled floor as he exploded out of it, holding his phone above his head with his thumb at its base. "That's it, I'm pressing publish, with or without your damn letters! Who the hell do you think you all are, calling my daughter janky?"

"Please, Eric! Don't do it! I'll find a way to get you them all!" Brady shouted.

"Too late! Now, get the hell out of here! All of you sons of bitches!"

The room emptied. In the end, it was only Mr. Brady who seemed overly bothered about the supposed publishing of his supposed dirty laundry. I rushed out of the room with the suits, hoping to vacate the premises before Caneer tried to further implicate me.

"Jennings, where do you think you're going?" I paused, watching the last of the suits enter the parking garage.

"Your work is far from done here." The cars reversed. Caneer closed the door. "Now we're going to really publish this shit. And we're going to add more, much more!"

"We are?" I said, looking at his chin.

"Damn straight."

I started to turn back towards the closet room, a little nervous about what Caneer might do if I refused.

"Well, shit, look at the time. I have to pick up Jenny from her social media video-making class."

I tried not to smile.

"How early can you be in here tomorrow?"

"Seven?"

"Make it six, Jennings."

"Sounds good," I said, opening the door to the garage.

On the way home, I stopped at a cell phone shop to get a new number. There was a liquor store across the street. I went in and bought a six-pack of Miller Light. Behind the till on a top rack was a bottle of rum next to a picture of Don the Beachcomber. "I'll take that bottle, too, please," I said, pointing to the picture of Don.

"What are you celebrating?" The shop attendant asked.

"Retirement."

Blonde Blind

She raised her hand as I idled past her in my cherry red Porsche. When she brought my espresso the following day, she asked my name.

"Duncan," I said, smiling, staring into her emerald eyes.

"I'm Samantha. Nice to meet you." She held out her lily-white hand.

I kissed it. "Oh, the pleasure is all mine, Samantha. How long have you been working here?"

The wind blew a tuft of her thick blonde hair over the side of her face. I noticed a small tattoo of a dagger below her ear.

She fixed her hair, saying, "For a while now. I was in the kitchen when I first started. I'm sorry it's taken me so long to introduce myself. I hear you've been coming here for a few months?"

"Every day for the last year or so."

"Oh, not that long?" she blushed, giggling.

"I normally ride the subway. It was probably the Porsche that caught your attention yesterday."

"Oh, I didn't even notice the Porsche." Her voice seemed to carry louder.

I looked down into my espresso, biting my tongue. The foam was a heart shape. Samantha stepped closer, touching her thigh against the table. A fruity fragrance crawled into my nose, a scent that reminded me of the sweaty laundry mats I'd frequented with my mom as a kid. I turned away from Samantha, coughing, then swooped my head into the steam of my coffee.

"It looks like a heart, doesn't it? It was supposed to be a cloud." She giggled again, less confident. "To accompany the weather." Her palms turned up towards the gloomy sky.

"Yes, I suppose."

A bell rang from inside the café, a purposeful dinging that sounded more like an alarm than the chime of a clock. "Oh, that's my manager. I had better run now." She craned her neck towards the direction of the bell, with her face tensed and her voice a little shaky. Before leaving, she placed her hand on my wrist. I felt a lovely warmth grip my insides. "Do give me a call, Duncan." On the back of the tab was a number, written in rose blush lipstick, and the outline of the same heart shape that had been floating in my coffee. I watched her walk turn into a prance just before she disappeared.

That night, I called my security guy. I asked him to run a background check on Samantha. "A Samantha who works at Sam and Sam's Coffeehouse, Lux. Got it?" I also provided him with the number she'd written on the napkin.

I sipped on a glass of Brandy, going in and out of a financial report published by Forbes Magazine. I'd read a few sentences, then pick up my phone, scanning my email apps, texts, and voicemail, making sure I hadn't missed anything. I called my guy back around midnight when I felt my eyes growing heavy.

"And? What'd you find, Lux?"

"About what, Sir?"

"Samantha!"

"Oh yes, the girl. Sorry, I was going to send you an update in the morning."

"Tell me now."

"She's as clean as a whistle, Mr. Cross."

He paused. "Is she blonde?"

"What's that got to do with anything?"

"I'm just looking out for you, Sir."

I hung up, shuffled to my oversized marble-tiled bathroom, and picked up my razor. I shaved my face, nose, and ears with a newfound attention to my appearance. As I was about to turn off my phone, as I'd done every night for twenty years, I thought of texting or calling Samantha. The nervous feeling in my stomach surprised me, the same feeling I'd get before signing a deal. I let the feeling pass, then turned off my phone and went to bed.

The next day, I drove my baby blue Maserati, idling back and forth in front of the coffeehouse, pretending to look for a parking space; my window rolled down. Samantha noticed me on my third drive-by. She was busy scribbling an order for a family of five when she dropped her leather-bound notebook onto the black table and waved her hands. "Duncan!" She shouted. "I'll have a table ready for you in a few seconds! There's a good parking spot over there!" She rushed to the small white picket fence and leaned over it, pointing to a spot near a green dumpster.

A short, stocky man wearing a blue tie greeted me at the entrance of the coffee shop. He had the same dagger tattoo as Samantha but on his wrist.

"Well, good morning, Mr. Cross; Samantha has a table ready for you. Follow me." I hadn't seen him before. As I trailed behind the man, trying not to think too hard about the tattoo's significance, I noticed a little bell in his back pocket. I caught a blast of Samantha's fruity perfume. Lifting my gaze, I rubbed my eyes as they began to water. "She loves that cheap crap, doesn't she?"

"Excuse me?" The strong, little man said, craning his neck, his eyebrows raised.

I couldn't see Samantha as I searched for her between the white-clothed tables spaced barely five feet apart.

"What was that, Mr. Cross?"

The short, little man had his shoulders squared to me now. I felt irritated that he'd stopped. I put my palm on his shoulder, nudging it. "Oh, nothing; carry on, would you."

When we turned the corner, I saw Samantha sitting down at a triangle-shaped table in a more private space. Her white and red buttoned shirt was buttoned at least two or three buttons lower than the previous day, revealing a delightful helping of lily-white cleavage.

"I wanted to join you today, Duncan. Is that okay?"

I looked down Samantha's shirt as she spoke, aware she could see me doing so. She didn't seem to care. She grabbed my hand and pulled me into the seat beside her.

"Well, I'd be offended if you didn't spend just a little time with me on this beautiful morning." I raised her hand to my chapped lips and kissed all the way up to her silver bracelet. I watched Samantha for any hint of uncomfortableness, a tug from her arm, a sliding of her chair. She remained, dare I say, in a state of blissful delight, staring into my eyes.

The manager stood between us, looking on like a red-light district peepshow observer with his arms folded, his nostrils flared, and his neck and head seemingly merged. "You can leave us now," I said, sharpening my eyes and tone.

"Oh yes, yes, of course. Excuse me, Mr. Cross. I'll bring you a little coffee and some breakfast soon."

I noticed Samantha making brief eye contact with the man, then she quickly returned her gaze to me.

The bull-built manager walked back to the entrance, turning his head to look at us every seven steps or so.

"So, what's the deal here?" I said, moving my chair a little away from hers.

She curled her hair behind her ears. "What do you mean, Duncan?"

"Oh, come on." I held out my hand towards the single rose on the table and scanned the coffee shop. "This. You. Him. I'm no fool."

She readjusted her position in her chair and dipped her gaze towards her knees. "I just thought we might get to know each other a little better, that's all."

Placing my hand on her knee, I squeezed gently. "I think you saw me riding in a Porsche, and now you want to get to know me a little better."

Samantha's big eyes widened. She scratched the back of her neck. She shifted her chair closer and looked around nervously. "Would you put your arm around me, Duncan?"

I didn't have a chance to respond as she lifted and then dropped my big arm around her paper-thin neck.

"If he sees us like this, he'll think it's all going according to plan."

"Going to plan?" I nudged backward, trying to pull my arm off her, but she squeezed and pulled on my hand.

"Please, just hear me out a minute, Duncan. Please." Her eyes were like the eyes of an animal in retreat.

There was something earnest in her voice, something I hadn't heard. I settled in my seat, relaxing my arm around her like we were lifetime lovers.

I smiled. "Go ahead, Samantha."

She moved her hand over my knuckles. "Thank you. About six months ago, Sam and I had to tap into our savings to keep this place going."

"You own this place?" I interrupted. "With him?"

"Yes. It's been bad for a while, a sinking ship."

I peered over her thick blonde head to see if Sam was watching. "So you're married to that little tough guy?"

"We're married, yes."

Flinching, I tried to pull my arm again.

"Please, hear me out, would you?"

She looked over her shoulder, then back at me, and continued, "He turned mean when the business started going bad. He started hitting me, taking our losses out on me, saying I'm not pulling my weight."

She stopped talking and hid her head in my chest. When she lifted it again, small tears ran down her cheeks. "We've been looking for someone like you for a while now."

"Someone like me?" I blurted out, moving my head back to see her clearer.

"Yes. Somebody rich. Somebody we could hustle. Men like you are easy to fool."

I felt my stomach twist into a knot. My teeth gnawed gently into my tongue.

"Oh, I don't mean you specifically, Duncan." Samantha looked closely at my mouth.

I released my tongue.

"Just rich men in general," she continued. "But I won't do it. As afraid as I am of him, I won't do it!" She grabbed my other hand, squeezed it, and placed it above her knee.

"So then, what exactly are we doing here?" I thought about removing my hand from her leg, but I liked the feeling of having it there.

"Buying me some time, that's all." She started crying again.

"So how was this supposed to go down? I just throw a bunch of money at you because you're pretty?"

Just then, Sam approached our table with a pen and notepad. "You lovebirds decide what you'd like to have?"

Samantha grabbed my sunglasses and casually put them on. "How do I look, boss? I've never worn a pair of Dolce and Gabbana's before."

I yanked my sunglasses off her head. In a reactionary instant, she slid my hand further up her leg, pushing it into her thigh. I was about to say something to Sam, calling him out, explaining I was fully aware of their attempted con. There was something in Samantha's eyes that stopped me, something like the look of a helpless, frightened child.

"On second thought, they suit you very nicely." I gently repositioned my shades over her eyes and kissed her cheek.

"We'll take two coffees and two breakfast burritos. That'll be all, Sam. Get on with it, would you."

When Sam disappeared behind the wall, Samantha took my hand from her leg and placed it between her tiny palms. "Thank you, Duncan."

She no longer seemed like the attractive waitress I hoped to wrap in my bedsheets. Her soft, hollow eyes were beginning to make me feel like I was the only person in the world who could help her.

"You know," I said. "I've solved much bigger problems in my illustrious career on Wall Street."

Samantha let go of my hand, lowering her gaze to her black Converse high tops. "This isn't your problem to solve, Duncan."

A screaming ambulance sped past, causing me to raise my voice. "Well, I'm not going to let that dickweed take advantage of you any longer!"

I pulled out my phone from my jacket pocket and searched my contacts. "The first thing we'll do is get you in touch with my old buddy, George. He's the best lawyer in town."

I expected Samantha's head to rise, and her face brighten, but my words seemed to make her even more sullen. She began flicking her shoelace as though it were an irritating fly.

"What's the matter?" I lifted her chin to look into her eyes.

"His dad's the presiding judge in these parts." She looked away from me into the street, her eyes wandering, not locked in on anything specific. "Don't worry about it, Duncan. You've been kind enough to buy me a little time here."

"So what exactly are you going to do then?"

Her gaze drifted back to mine. "I'm not entirely sure yet. Maybe jump on a plane to Mexico." She laughed, a nervous, scared laugh.

I watched her eyes narrow, then move to something behind me. I put my palm on Samantha's hand.

"Two burritos and the freshest coffee this side of the Mississippi. Anything else I can get for you two?"

I wanted to drive my fist into Sam's sternum.

"That'll be all," I said, staring at my underwhelmingly thin burrito, nervous I'd knock him out if I glanced too long into his eyes.

"Well, just shout if you need anything."

I could tell he'd disappeared behind the wall when Samantha's expression softened.

"You ever been to Mexico?"

The coffee cup covered most of her face as she tilted it back to take a sip. She almost dropped it when the hot liquid touched her tongue. "No, the furthest south I ever went was Florida. I was just joking, though. I'd never really do something like that."

I picked up her dainty hand and placed it between my palms. "Why not?"

"I'm a scaredy-cat, for one. And I got no more than a few hundred dollars to my name for two."

She blushed and smiled with what I thought was a little embarrassment in her eyes.

"Here's what we're going to do. I've got a holiday house in El Dorado. It's a beautiful spot, right on the beach. I'm a member of a private club down there. You're going to board my plane tonight and spend a few weeks down there while I figure out how to get you out of this mess..." I paused, turning to look back to the front of the coffee house. "I'm going to make damn sure that excuse of a man never takes advantage of you ever again."

Samantha placed her other hand on top of mine, moving it back and forth over my knuckles. "Oh, Duncan, I couldn't accept that. I'll figure my way out of this." She quickly removed her hand and stared absently into the busy street. "Somehow."

"Well, I won't accept no for an answer." I pulled out my phone and texted my assistant.

"Here's how it's going to go down. We're going to leave together, arm in arm. Dickweed over there will think it's all going according to plan. Then I'll have my driver pick you up and take you to the airport. In two weeks, I'll come and see you, and we'll assess the situation."

Samantha's expression seemed to soften. "Really?" She said, placing her hand back on mine.

"Already done."

"I'll need a few hours, Duncan, but I promise I'll do it."

I nodded. Samantha moved closer, stood, whispered in my ear, then kissed me on the cheek.

*

We texted each other twice a day over the next two weeks. Samantha sent me photos of her lounging by the pool, on the beach, and sipping glasses of wine. Her texts always included the red lips emoji, and *I can't wait to see you, Duncan.*

On the valet ride from the airport to the club, I tried calling Samantha. When it went to voicemail twice, I tried calling the landline at my house, but the result was the same. I told my driver, Vinny, to stop at the security shack. I handed a 24-pack of local beer to Miguel, the security guard.

"Miguel," I said, "You seen that pretty little, blonde girl over the last two weeks or so? Her name's Samantha. She's staying at my place."

"Yes, yes, Mr. Duncan. Very nice people. Very nice. But messy. And brown hair, no?"

"You mean person," I replied, showing a single finger. "And that color is blonde, close to yellow."

I felt a little bad, knowing how hard Miguel had worked to improve his English over the years.

Miguel frowned. "But."

And then, raising two fingers, he chuckled, "There are two of them—a miss and a mister. And her hair is the same color as mine—brown."

"What?" I shouted, flashbacks of the coffeehouse stabbing into my mind.

"A strong-looking short man?" I extended my elbows away from my body as though holding two watermelons.

"Si. Si, Mr. Duncan."

I opened the door on the driver's side of the big black SUV, shouting, "Move!"

Vinny didn't seem to hear me, sitting motionless in his seat. I grabbed his hand and yanked on it, almost sending him face-first into the concrete.

"Mr. Duncan, please, what's the matter?"

I slammed the door, put my foot on the gas, and blew through every stop sign en route to my home. Everything was in shambles as I entered through the front gate of my property. My beautiful row of guava trees was charred black. My giant marble statue of the queen of Sheba lay on its side; her head cracked off her neck as though somebody had methodically decapitated her. The front teak door, wide open, had a giant chunk missing, which I found on the floor, resting on top of my Antique Blue Mid 19th-century Persian rug, stained in a god-awful red-purple death-like color.

I left Mexico before dawn the next day, trying my best to concentrate on my breath when two sleeping pills couldn't knock me out for the duration of the flight. When I arrived home, I changed into loose-fitting athletic apparel. I caught the subway and got out at the closest stop to the coffee shop. When I walked in, a young-looking, rail-thin boy greeted me.

"I'm looking for Sam and Samantha," I mumbled in a deliberately low voice.

"The owner? Yes, I'll go get him."

I followed the kid into the kitchen; my firsts curled into sharp-knuckled balls.

An older man smoking a cigarette stopped me as I pushed through the double swinging doors. "Yes, I'm Sam. What do you want?"

Scouring the kitchen like a bird of prey, I searched for Sam and Samantha, not making eye contact with the boy or the old man.

"What the hell do you want?" The man stepped in front of me.

"Where's Samantha and that short, pudgy prick?"

The boy's eyes went nervy. He slipped back through the swinging doors.

"Oh shit." The old man grabbed a dish rag and began wiping the counter behind him. "You got ripped off, didn't you?"

The man wouldn't look at me in the eyes. "They only worked here for a few weeks—a Suzy and Rodney Fletcher. Those are the names the cops gave me when they came in the other day. But they were already long gone. Been doing this throughout the country, scamming older, richer men for whatever they can get. Sorry, man. I'll take your number and let you know when the cops notify me of anything."

I sat at the table where Samantha and I had spent breakfast together. I could almost smell her cheap perfume, still ruining the air.

"What the hell?" I whispered, scratching the scruff on my chin, watching a tall blonde walk her poodle across the street.

Baby Can't Fly

Mr. Tony squeezed Nick's shoulders until the jackhammer stopped. "There's a man in a suit looking for you. You got five minutes, kid."

Sprinting across the construction yard, Nick tried to recall any outstanding debts. None came to mind.

"You Nick Sellers?" The black-suited man stood almost as tall as the gate, leaning into the chain-linked fence with his arms stretched above him. Nick stared at the man's gold Rolex. "Who's asking?"

Grinning, the man replied, "Don't worry, you're not in trouble, kid. Far from it."

The tall man began fiddling with the lock, humming loudly.

"How'd you know that song?" Nick's green eyes softened as his shoulders settled below his long, thin neck.

"My name's Mel Gantz. I hate to use such a cliché, but I'm a big-time Nashville executive, and I like your stuff, kid."

"Time's up! Get back to work, Sellers!" Mr. Tony shouted across the yard.

Nick grabbed a key from his pocket and opened the gate. "I got to get back to work."

Mel laughed, cupping Nick's shoulder with his massive hand, "Tell Gonzo over there you're quitting. I got a twenty-thousand-dollar check with your name on it. We'll call it a little sign-on bonus."

Nick paused, trying to hide his involuntary smile. Approaching the jackhammer, he noticed his grizzly grey-haired foreman, charging.

"I sure hope you're paying for this kid's time, 'cause I sure ain't! Not for standing around and scratching his balls!" Mr. Tony removed his hard hat and safety goggles. His small blue eyes had red-veiny strands streaking out the sides. Mel lifted Nick's hand. He shook it. He picked up the radio, resting on the workbench. "Nick doesn't work for you anymore, Gonzo. You'll be hearing him on your radio soon."

Mr. Tony laughed, yanking the radio out of Mel's hand. "Good riddance."

Turning Nick from Mr. Tony, Mel led the young blonde-haired musician out of the yard. Nick didn't hesitate, didn't even think to go back and collect his lunchbox and water bottle.

"Where's your car, kid?"

Nick stood with his hands in his pockets, examining Mel's black Lexus. "I ride the bus."

Mel moved towards his Lexus and opened the backdoor. As Nick clipped on his seatbelt, Mel said, "Now let's go find Josie."

When the engine fired, Nick and Josie's lead single, "Baby Can't Fly," blared through a souped-up sound system. Nick cupped his ears with his hands.

"Sorry about that." Mel turned the volume down. "Can you tell I'm a fan? Those lyrics, though. My God."

Shifting to the middle seat, Nick leaned forward. "She wrote everything," he paused. "We broke up just a few months ago."

"What?" Mel turned to look at him, swerving into the emergency lane, almost hitting a cyclist. The car stopped, a small dust cloud enveloped the Lexus. Mel switched off the radio. "You're kidding?"

Nick didn't say anything, looking down the paint-stained pant legs of his dungarees.

"Right? Good joke, kid!"

Tracing his finger over the anchor tattoo on his wrist, Nick looked up at Mel. "She said I had to choose between her or the music."

"Where is she?"

"Still at her place on Tennington."

The car started up again. Mel pulled out his phone and placed it on his dashboard's charging dock. "What's the address, kid?"

"There's no use, Mr. Gantz."

"You giving up that easy?"

"She ain't signing anything to do with a music career, I'm telling you, Mr. Gantz. It doesn't matter how big the check is."

There was a brief silence, panned on the left by cars speeding by. Nick reached for the door handle, but

Mel's finger slammed onto the lock button. Mel removed his sunglasses and turned to face Nick with a joker's grin. "Who's got the rights to the songs, kid?"

One of Mel's blue eyes had a slight grey tinge to it. Nick stared deeply into it, searching for something to trust. "What do you mean?"

"Who owns them?"

"We both do, I guess," Nick said with a shaky lack of confidence.

"Do you love her?"

"I've never stopped loving her." Nick let go of the door handle.

"Well, that's exactly what you'll tell her."

Looking out the window, Nick's eyes searched for something. "I'm not doing that to her again. No way."

Mel opened the glove compartment, grabbed a check, and set it down on the middle console, face up, so Nick could see it. "Love's just a game, kid."

Nick picked up the check and read it. "I thought you said twenty-thousand."

"What's another thirty? Once we get going, you'll be making five times more than this. Give me the word, and I'll drive you back to that construction site, and you can keep working for Gonzo."

Nick set the check back down. "So what, I'm just supposed to go back to her and tell her I love her? Tell her that I don't care about the music? And then what? She'll just welcome me back with open arms?"

Mel turned the radio on and then touched Nick's shoulder. "We're going to figure it out together. The only thing I can promise is that the both of you are going to be better for it. You got a gift—both of you—and it's time the world hears it. The first thing you'll do is tell her you're sorry and that you made the biggest mistake of your life. That'll be it for now. One step at a time, kid."

Josie's harmonies did something to Nick's otherwise average-sounding voice, pulling it up to someplace he couldn't reach himself. And while new melodies came to him as often as he tied his mud-crusted work boots, Josie's lyrics gave the songs a timeless edge, as though they'd always existed. Over the volume of the music and the cars still racing past, Nick raised his voice, "Forty-one Tennington Place."

Mel parked five houses away from Josie's and handed Nick a few hundred dollar bills and his business card. "Call me tonight. This should hold you over for a while."

Stuffing the bills into his pocket, Nick kept his eyes on the check on the middle console.

"Hey kid, how many more songs you got?"

"At least fifty."

Mel smiled, folded the check, and returned it to the glove compartment.

"Get the girl, and you'll get the cash, kid. It's as simple as that."

Walking past the bed of marigolds up the stairs to Josie's front door, Nick felt a wave of anxiety crash over his insides. He stopped to rethink it all. He scanned the area for Mel's black Lexus, but Mel had already driven off.

"What the hell you doing here?" The front door opened.

"Josie." Nick stepped closer, moved by the flutter in his stomach. "You look beautiful." There was a short pause. Nick's tone became more intense, "I was wrong. About everything. I'm so sorry, Josie."

Josie pushed on the door a little, so Nick could only see from her neck. "It's too late."

Her big black eyes were even more perfectly round than he remembered. She'd cut her hair since he'd last seen her. He used to make her promise that she'd never shorten it. This new hairstyle made her look older. Nick didn't mind. It was enough just seeing one strand of her thick as honey-like hair touch her small, delicate shoulders. "The new look suits you," he said, staring at her hair. The door slammed shut.

"Josie. Josie, please."

Nick beat his palm on Josie's door for a good minute, then walked home, biting on his bottom lip. After downing three shots of Vodka, the last of an old bottle his mom bought him for Christmas, he called Mel. "It's no use, Mr. Gantz. I'm telling you, she wants nothing to do with me."

There was a short silence. Mel firmed up his tone. "You're going to go back there tomorrow with her favorite bouquet. You're going to tell her you're sorry. And then you're going to do that again and again and again—until you've won her back. And in the meantime, pick up your guitar and start practicing."

Staring at the empty bottle of Vodka, listening to Gantz, Nick wished he had another bottle. "It's not that easy, Mr. Gantz. You don't know her like I do. She's stubborn. And I hurt her, cut her so deep. I'm telling you, she won't change her mind."

There was another short pause, and then Mel spoke much calmer. "Well, the way I see it, you've only got two options. Give up on your music career and Josie, and ask Gonzo for your job back. Or believe me. Believe what I believe."

"Which is what exactly?" Nick stammered.

"That you've got something, a real shot at making it."

Per Mel's guidance, Nick knocked on Josie's door again the next day with a big bouquet of sunflowers. The result was the same, except on this occasion, Josie didn't even open the door, shouting at him through the keyhole, warning that she'd call the cops if he didn't vacate the premises. Nick called Mel that night, but Mel's message remained the same. "Love's just a game, kid. Get the girl, you get the cash."

As the days and rejections piled up, Nick thought about calling Mr. Tony and asking for his job back, but with every real consideration came a slip of cash from Mel, holding Nick over for a short while and always with an unwavering reassurance, "Stick to the plan, kid. You're close. Trust me."

"Maybe we don't need Josie?" Nick said on one occasion. "Or we can find somebody with a similar voice to hers."

Mel didn't budge. "It's Josie and Nick or Nick and Gonzo. Stick to the plan, kid."

The turning point eventually came on Nick's tenth time walking up Josie's stairs. Her name wasn't yet out of his mouth when Josie opened the door. She hadn't put on her makeup yet, a look he preferred. He stood, staring, confused by her beautiful but warm, inviting expression.

"You won't ever give up, will you?"

Dazed, Nick said nothing, standing, staring.

"It's what I always loved about you. Such a dangerous thing, though."

"Why?" Nick asked, snapping out of his catatonic state.

"Because there are some things worth giving up on."

"Not you." Stepping forward, Nick touched Josie's small lily-white hand. "I haven't picked up a guitar since you left."

"It can't be the way it was, Nick. It won't work."

"I know," he said softly.

"Not how it consumed you. You treated me like I was just another instrument in the studio."

Letting go of Josie's hand, Nick broke eye contact and tilted his head downward. "I made everything about the music. Even us, the only thing that's ever mattered."

Josie grabbed Nick's hand, pulling him over the door threshold and into her arms. "Do you still have those sunflowers?"

Nick's steps home that night carried a clash of bliss and uneasy guilt. He buried his internal conflict with humming, and then, with a complete disregard for being heard, he belted out, "My baby can't fly 'cause her wings got burnt by red-hot desire!" Before bed that night, Nick checked his phone and saw ten missed calls from Mr. Gantz. Just as he'd resolved to call back Gantz in the morning, his phone lit up again.

"I was just about to call you, Mr. Gantz."

"What took you so long, kid? You forget our arrangement that fast?" Mel spoke quickly and firmly with a pointed tone.

Nick kept silent.

"And? How'd it go today? Any better? You order her dinner like I said?"

"Getting closer."

It was Mel's turn to collect his thoughts in the silence. *The kid doesn't call me. He's not bitching about her like he usually does. And I'll be damned if he doesn't sound a little happier tonight.*

Pressing his mouth to the speaker, Mel whispered, "You got her, didn't you, kid?"

"I can't go through with it! I won't do that to her again!" Nick shouted, an anxious shrill.

"Whoa, whoa, slow down, kid. This is the kind of news worth celebrating. I'll be at your place in twenty minutes."

Mel hung up before Nick could speak another word. He tried calling Mr. Gantz three times, but the call went to voicemail.

Nick woke up when Mel's car horn blared in his driveway an hour later. The first thing he saw when he opened the car door was Mel's hand on top of a pile of cash on the middle console.

"You ready to have some fun?" Mel split the pile of cash and handed one half to Nick. "Call it a final piece

215

of the puzzle bonus, kid. Just another taste of what's coming your way."

Nick moved his fingers across the cash like it was a fine silk cloth.

"You like gambling?"

Nick studied Mel's perfectly ironed pair of black capris and the brightest Aloha shirt he'd ever seen.

"Love it," Nick replied, still feeling waves of euphoria from the touch of the cash.

"What's your game?"

"Blackjack." Nick smiled.

"Ah, I figured you were more of a poker guy. I know just the place for a good game of blackjack."

When they pulled into the pink-lit parking lot of The Hotel Flamingo, Nick was still gripping his pile of cash with vice grip hands.

"You can leave that here, kid. We'll use this stack for the table." Mel showed his half of the cash, and opened the glove compartment. Nick nervously stuffed his money into it.

Mel greeted three pretty girls at the front desk by name. He led Nick through a dark, grimy kitchen into a red-lit backroom guarded by a big bald man with a half-eaten sandwich tattooed on his head.

"Mr. Gantz, nice to see you again. What's the occasion?" The man held out his gorilla hand.

Mel put his arm around Nick and then shook the man's hand. "This kid's about to be famous, Nibbler."

Smiling, the big man bent to get eye level with Nick. "You must be good, kid. Mr. Gantz, don't waste his time with no jokers. What's the name?"

"Nick Cunningham."

"Nick and Josie!" Mel shouted, stepping in front of Nick, "Be listening, Nibbler!"

As they crossed the threshold, Nick felt a chill run down his spine hearing Josie's name, considering even for a second trying to convince her to get back into the game.

"Here, kid, go start at the table over there." Mel handed Nick three hundred dollar bills. Nick instantly snapped back into the present moment. Besides the dealer, there was only one other person at the blackjack table: an old lady puffing on what looked like just the glow of a cigarette. She didn't move her gaze from the deck of cards in her hand. "You must be pretty good, kid."

Nick turned to look at her and inhaled a small cloud of smoke. Coughing, he managed, "I don't play much."

"I don't mean blackjack, kid. We all know what it means when Gantz brings in somebody like you."

"Hit," Nick said to the dealer, then turned to the old lady. "What does it mean?"

"That's a bad hit, kid." The lady looked at Nick with a mean stare, placed her cards face down, pushed her cigarette into the astray, then got up and walked away.

By the time Gantz came round to the blackjack table, Nick had managed to turn his three hundred into four hundred.

"I see you're treating him right, Solly!" Gantz raised his shot glass to the dealer.

"The kid knows how to play!"

Gantz played a couple of hands with Nick and the dealer. After a short while, he placed his hand on the main deck of cards. "Mind giving us a few minutes, Solly?"

"Not a problem, sir." Solly put the cards underneath the table, removed his gloves, then walked away.

A red-haired waitress walked by. Gantz grabbed a bottle of Beluga Gold Line off her tray, then poured a shot into his and Nick's glasses. "I think I've figured out how you can make it without her, without ruining your relationship. I can see you love her, kid."

Nick slung the shot of Vodka into his mouth like it was a sip of water. "Really? How?"

Reaching into his pocket, Mel pulled out a folder and placed it on the table. "She's just got to sign a few lines of this document. You'll get a hundred grand to share."

Nick straightened in his seat, the look of excitement in his glazed eyes. "For just a couple of signatures? And we don't have to rope her into any performance or anything like that?"

Gantz put his hand on Nick's shoulder and squeezed. "I'm going to make it work, kid."

On the drive home, Nick asked Gantz for three weeks before approaching Josie for her signature.

Gantz sighed, conceding, "Well, that's fine, kid. But not a day later. I'll keep the document until then."

"It's just that I want to be sure she knows I'm not using her, Mr. Gantz. I'll do it, I promise. I think I can get her to agree."

Nick didn't hear much from Gantz over the next three weeks, just the occasional text and phone call. He and

Josie spent every waking hour together, holding hands, laughing, and staying up late kissing until the fire turned to coals. One day, Nick picked up his guitar and showed Josie a new melody he'd come up with.

"Keep playing," she said with a wide smile and a glow in her eyes. She left the living room for a minute. When she returned, she had her notebook open and began singing, "We're both the same, you and me, chasing yesterday's dreams with dirt on our feet."

"Yeah, that's it, Josie!" Nick shouted, strumming louder and singing with her. He stopped playing once they'd smoothed it out, setting his guitar down and embracing her. "You've got a gift, Josie. A real gift."

She smiled, kissing him on the cheek. "You know I don't like you talking like that."

"But it's true. You got to be doing something with it."

Josie backed away from Nick, turning her gaze to the window. "I write because I love it, not because I want to get something out of it."

There was a short silence. Josie shifted closer to Nick again. "I guess we're just different in that way." Josie put her hand in Nick's. "I saw how it consumed you, Nick, how it consumed us. I don't want that again."

Nick ran his fingers back and forth from her wrist up to her forearm. "I think I've found a way for this music thing to work. For both of us."

"What?" Josie flinched, yanking her arm to her side.

Nick noticed the panic on her face, her eyes creasing, her lips tightening.

"Just hear me out, Jo. And if it doesn't sit right, then no bother." Nick paused, tracking Josie's eyes, watching her observe the passing cars out the window.

"What is it?," she whispered.

"I met a man willing to give us a hundred grand for our songs."

Josie turned from the window and landed her sharp eyes on Nick. "Not this again, Nick. I can't do it!"

Clutching Josie's hand, Nick moved closer to her. "Wait," he said. "Hear me out. We don't have to do anything, Josie. No performing, no recording. We just have to sign a few documents."

Josie wriggled her hand out of Nick's grasp.

Nick stood, turning towards the door. "I got to believe, Jo, that there's something more for us. But I'm not going to hurt you again. I promise you that." He turned back to Josie, clutched her hand, and placed it on his chest.

Sensing sadness, not anger, in Nick's soft voice, Josie stood. "I'll read over the document."

"Thank you," he replied. He opened the front door.

Just as Nick had crossed the threshold, Josie smiled, "Hey, Nick." she said. He turned to look at her. "Yeah."

"There's nothing more we'll ever need than what we've got right now."

She blew him a kiss. "I'll see you later."

That night, before going to bed, Nick called Mr. Gantz.

"Well, this is a nice surprise, kid. I thought you'd gone back to work for Gonzo!"

Nick opened the pantry cupboard above his microwave and pulled out a brand-new bottle of Titos. "I think she's gonna sign, Mr. Gantz."

"What!?"

Nick yanked the phone from his eardrum, frightened by the volume from Gantz. With a much slower, softer delivery, Gantz continued, "Yeah, I mean, I was expecting that, kid. Uh, why wouldn't she sign, you know?"

The Vodka burned the back of Nick's throat.

"But she wants to read the document first."

"For what!?" Gantz blurted.

"Ah, I guess…"

"Well, just tell me, is this Josie of yours a pretty clever girl, kid?" Gantz asked, interrupting Nick.

"The smartest girl I ever met."

There was a short silence. Nick stared at the bottle of Titos, deciding whether or not to pour another shot.

"And the prettiest, too," he said, smiling.

"Well, you've already put me out a little more time and money than I initially expected, kid. By the time Josie reads and signs the documents, we would've missed our window." Gantz's voice was much more recollected and a little muffled, as though he was pressing his mouth right up into the phone speaker.

The warm, euphoric feeling disappeared from Nick as quickly as Gantz had finished speaking. "Well, please now, Mr. Gantz. We're so very close here."

Gantz opened the Mustangs of America calendar on his desk. "I'm giving you until the end of the day tomorrow, kid. If I don't get the signed document back with both your signatures, it'll be back to Gonzo for you. I'll drop the papers off at your place in the morning."

On his walk to Josie's house the next day, Nick read through the Gantz document five times, each attempt resulting in no more clarity than the former. Josie's front door was wide open when he arrived.

"Josie? You home?"

He walked up the stairs and opened her bedroom door to find her on her bed wearing her big set of headphones, pen in hand, and journal in her lap. He tapped her on the shoulder. She jumped backward in fright but came closer to him just as quickly, kissing him on the cheek and removing her headphones.

"You're getting the itch again, aren't you?" Nick smiled.

"It never left," Josie replied, smiling back at him.

Moving to Josie's desk, Nick grabbed a pen and placed it and Gantz's document in Josie's hands, pointing to the bottom line. "Look, Jo, a hundred grand. All we have to do is sign."

Josie spent a minute reading the document before putting it face-down on her bed.

"How long have you had this document?"

Nick didn't say anything.

"I'm not signing it."

"What? Why?" Nick picked up the document and scanned it, trying to find something he'd missed.

"He's going to take all the rights to our songs. The writing and publishing."

Dropping the document back onto Josie's bed, Nick moved closer to her, staring into her eyes with a blank face.

"He'll own our songs, Nick. He'll be able to edit and do whatever the hell he wants with them!"

"But Josie," Nick said anxiously, clutching her hand. "For a hundred grand. That's a down payment on a house!"

Josie jumped off her bed, turning to Nick before heading down the stairs to the backdoor in the kitchen. "Those songs are a part of me. I won't sell them for all the money in the world!"

Nick felt his stomach churn with anger and desperation. He imagined returning to work at the construction yard, immediately feeling like he might puke. Picking up the document, he ran after Josie, shouting, "You're so damn selfish! Always have been! Finally, we get a damn break, but you can't see it, too blinded by your damn ego and pride!"

Josie sat down next to the bird feeder, slow tears running down her cheeks. She began wiping out the tray. She held out her hand, staring at Nick until he handed her the document. "You'll never be happy, Nick, never be satisfied in the simple joy of creating without some big payout or fame." She dried her face with her shirt, standing, her eyes turning from the document, and now staring at him sternly. Just as he thought she was about to sign it, she stepped closer to him.

"And then, if you ever make it, whatever that means, you'll only want more! Until it bleeds out every bit of your soul!" Josie pointed to the last line of the document, the place for their signatures and the date. "Do you think I'm stupid? This contract is dated the same day you began knocking on my door." Josie began jabbing her finger into Nick's chest. "You've played me for a fool, Nick!"

Nick stepped back, placing his hand over the area of his chest she'd been stabbing. "Will you just think about it, Jo? We have until the end of the day to sign."

"There I was, thinking you'd changed!" Josie screamed. "Never again! Get out!"

"But Jo…"

"Now!"

As Nick trudged home, a great weight of sadness, guilt, and shame lay heavy on his shoulders. He filled his coffee mug with Vodka, downed it in two sips. He called Gantz, wiping the tears from his eyes. "She's not signing, Mel." Nick began to cry. Mel said nothing. "I've ruined any chance of a future with her."

Nick could hear giggling in the background and some girls' voices. "Baby can't fly, I guess." Gantz laughed. "You gave it a good go, kid. I bet you can get on Gonzo's payroll again. Call me if anything changes. I'll be seeing you around." The phone clicked. "Mr. Gantz?"

The following morning, with a head pounding and full of static, Nick returned to the construction yard. He arrived just as Mr. Tony exited his black Toyota pickup truck.

"Well, look who it is! The radio king himself!" Mr. Tony smiled unnaturally like a clown.

"I was wondering if I could get my job back, Mr. Tony? I'm really sorry for running out on you like that."

Mr. Tony removed his set of keys from his belt buckle and unlocked the gate. Nick followed him into the yard —a red shipping container stored all the tools, heavy equipment, and miscellaneous items. Mr. Tony unlocked it and stepped inside, still not saying a word.

A nauseating feeling began in Nick's stomach as he observed the yard and the crew's progress.

"I knew you'd be back, kid." Mr. Tony came out of the container and handed Nick his lunchbox and water bottle.

"I'll start you at a dollar less than you were making before you ran out on me."

Mr. Tony turned on his stereo as usual, readying for the day. One of Nick's favorite tunes blared across the speakers. It made Nick feel worse. He stood up and grabbed the jackhammer. "Okay, if I get an early start?"

Mr. Tony smiled, a genuine smile, and then he handed Nick a hard hat, "Go for it, kid."

"Baby, can't fly," Nick muttered, then switched on the jackhammer and began pounding the ground.

Circus Sam

I moved to a new school in the eighth grade. Dad thought we needed a fresh start after mom died. It took my classmates one week to devise a nickname for me— one week of observing my zinc-painted face.

"You're just missing the green hair and juggling balls, Circus Sam!"

The first day Dad put the sunscreen on my face, I tried to wash it off before the morning bell, but the stuff was so thick I only made it worse, smearing it all down my neck. Then, when Dad picked me up after school, he quickly applied another coat, saying, "Looks like we didn't use enough this morning!"

Making it through the school day wasn't half as bad as the after-school pick-up. There weren't teachers on the curb, so I'd have to wait for Dad never less than forty-five minutes, and sometimes until dark.

Everybody stared, pointed, and laughed at me. Even the kids too shy to speak would look at me like I was from another planet, making sure they were at least ten feet away. Dad was always drunk or close to drunk when he picked me up, always with the same excuse,

"Sorry, Sam, that business meeting ran later than I thought."

We moved to a new town a week after Mom's funeral. The doctors found what they first called a "sunspot" on her shoulder. Six months later, that spot had grown into melanoma and spread to other parts of her body. She didn't have long after that.

Dad's initial response was heavy drinking. Then he stopped shaving, making his bed, doing the laundry, and washing the dishes. Some nights, maybe five a month, he'd ask me to sit down and have dinner with him. He'd try to cook something special, like steaks on the grill or the chicken and mushroom dish Mom used to make, but inevitably, something would burn, and I'd have to throw a frozen pizza in the microwave.

The dinners we'd eat together almost always ended with Dad in tears, slurring, "How's that bottle of sunscreen looking? Do we need more? I hope you're wearing a hat and sitting away from the window, right?"

I'd nod, "I'm okay. I promise."

"You've got your mother's skin, Sam. And she wasn't damn well okay!"

He'd proceed to inspect my body. "What the hell's that?"

"What?" I'd say, tracking his eyes.

"Is that a sunspot?"

I'd flick off a piece of food or show him it was just an innocent freckle.

At the end of my first week of school, a ninth-grade teacher, Mr. Stone, announced during our assembly that he'd be starting after-school tennis lessons, which I saw as an easy escape from the dreaded after-school wait for Dad.

I rushed to the stage once Mr. Stone had finished giving the announcement.

"I'd like to sign up, please."

He scratched his black stubbled chin, examining my clown-white face. Tilting my shoulders back and straightening my neck, I tried to make myself look athletic.

"You ever played before?"

"Yes." I lied.

"Get a signature from your parent, and bring a water bottle, non-marking shoes, and sun…" He paused, moving his eyes between my cheeks. He then handed me a piece of paper, which I folded and placed in my shirt pocket.

Dad was supposed to make BBQ ribs that night, but stayed in his room with the door locked. I tried knocking, but couldn't bang my fist hard enough to make a sound louder than his TV. I smiled when I opened the filing cabinet, remembering Mom's meticulous and organized manner. I grabbed an insurance form and scanned it for Dad's signature. It was relatively easy to copy, more or less a heart-shaped squiggle. I saw a photo when I returned the document to the folder. It was their wedding day. They were kissing, heads turned away from the camera. I stared at the photo, noting every detail: mom's white flower-laced dress, dad's black tuxedo with a blue bow tie, and their eyes, open and looking at each other as though they were the last two people in the world.

After school the next day, a few other kids and I sat waiting for Mr. Stone under an umbrella on white plastic chairs. When he arrived, he asked for our consent forms. I felt a little nervous when I handed it to him, but he didn't look twice, stuffing it into his tan briefcase.

"Everybody needs to put a little sunscreen on before we head out there. And don't be shy. You can never apply too much on a day like this."

I felt the stares, but nobody laughed. We followed Mr. Stone onto the court.

"Alright, two easy laps around the outside of the lines. No cheating!"

There were five of us—two boys I recognized from my grade and two girls a little older. When we'd finished our laps, we formed a semicircle in front of Mr. Stone and followed his instructions in a stretching routine.

"I want each of you to tell me your name and one thing you want to get from these classes."

One of the boys stopped touching his toes, standing straight.

"Now, I didn't say to stop stretching, though, you hear," Mr. Stone said, his palms flat on the cement.

"I'm John, and I'm not that good at anything, so I decided to try tennis."

Mr. Stone immediately stood up, approached John, and shook his hand.

"I'm glad you're here, John."

"My name's Nicole. My grandma was an excellent tennis player. She died last year."

I felt my heart beating faster as each kid shared their name and reason for attending. We were on our backs, stretching our hamstrings when it came to my turn.

"My name's Sam. I'm new, and I, uh, I really like tennis."

"We're glad you're here, Sam. Aren't we?"

I couldn't see Mr. Stone's face as he spoke because my eyes were closed, blinded by the sun, but I felt the warmth of his voice.

"Aren't we?" He said again, a little more sternly.

The other kids all responded, "Yes, welcome. Welcome, Sam."

It was the first time I'd heard my new peers call me by my name without putting *circus* before it.

None of us had rackets, so after stretching and introducing ourselves, we picked a racket from the pile next to the net post.

"Not that one, Sam. That's an inch or two too small for you."

"Oh yeah, of course," I said, not looking at Mr. Stone.

I then suspected he realized I'd never played before, but it didn't seem to matter to him.

"Here, this one's perfect for you."

Mr. Stone handed me a green racket with a soft, brown leather grip.

We formed a line at what Mr. Stone called the baseline. He showed us how to hit a forehand and a backhand, then gave us two attempts at each shot before we circled to the back of the line. None of us got more than a quarter of our attempts within the lines that day, but whenever we did, Mr. Stone sprang to his feet, removing his sunglasses, and cheered with his two fists raised above his head. His energy and vigor quickly became contagious, and we started copying him whenever one of us succeeded.

During the last five minutes of practice, we collected all the balls we'd hit over the fence, which must have been at least half of Mr. Stone's basket. I lingered behind the other kids as they left the court. Mr. Stone was zipping his bag and collecting his rackets when I squeezed some sunscreen out of his bottle and quickly lathered it all over my face.

He must have seen me walking away when he shouted, "Goodbye, Sam. You did good today, kid."

I had my back turned to him. I raised my hand and began jogging towards the pick-up area. I waited fifteen minutes before Dad arrived.

When I got into the car, Dad's eyes narrowed.

"What have you been doing?"

"What do you mean?"

"You've been sweating? God, Sam, don't tell me you've been out in the sun."

I stared out the window. "You've been drinking."

My heart began racing when I saw Mr. Stone approaching. I could tell he'd recognized me.

"They're about to close the gate. Drive!" I shouted, avoiding eye contact with Mr. Stone, tugging on the steering wheel in Dad's hands.

We started moving.

"Relax!" They're not going to lock us in!"

In the rearview mirror, I saw Mr. Stone turn around.

"I just want to get home."

"Now, don't lie to me. What were you doing out in the sun?"

"It was just a quick game of tag with some new friends, and most of it was under that big willow tree."

Dad grabbed my hand and glanced at my face. "Well, it looks like your face is still nicely covered."

We came to a stop at a red light. Dad leaned forward in his seat, turning his body towards me. "I'm glad you're making friends, Sam. I know this hasn't been easy for you. Once we get into the fall, we can ease back on the sunscreen."

He put his hand on my knee. "I haven't been there for you. I know. It's just…"

The light turned green.

"It's okay, Dad," I said. "I'm okay."

The next day at lunch, a boy tapped me on the shoulder. It was John.

"You coming to tennis?"

I smiled, "Yes, you?"

"Of course! Mind if I sit with you for lunch?"

"Please." I said.

I liked that John didn't ask me about the sunscreen on my face. We shared a packet of chips. Moments before the bell rang, a few boys started heckling us. "Look! It's Circus Sam and Jackass John! You boys need a little privacy to make out?!"

"Don't pay them any attention."

John stood up and began walking away. I didn't move at first.

"C'mon, Sam." John stopped, waiting for me.

I packed my lunch box into my backpack and then walked with him back to the classroom.

When I exited my classroom at the end of the day, John was waiting for me in the hallway. We walked to the tennis court together, guessing how many shots we'd make, admitting that we hoped to see Mr. Stone as animated as the day before.

Stepping down the long flight of stairs, I paid attention to how the court lay in relation to the road surrounding it. There was no way that Dad would see me if he drove by. The court was sunken, almost shielded in by the school grounds.

We hit a few less balls over the fence by the end of the second day's practice. Mr. Stone stopped us early and sat us down in the shady, grassy area outside the court.

"Tennis is a lot like life. You can't win every point. You're not going to make every shot. The best players know how to lose. They know how to get back up again."

I pretended to look for something in my backpack while the other kids left, including John, who offered to wait for me multiple times. Then, just as Mr. Stone began to wrap the chain-lock around the tennis court entrance door, I dabbed a big clunk of sunscreen into my hand. I didn't look back or hear him say goodbye as I hurried from the court to the after-school pick-up spot. Within only a few yards, I felt a hand on my shoulder.

"Was that your dad who picked you up yesterday, Sam?"

Mr. Stone lifted his hand and began walking a little ahead of me, craning his neck slightly to look me in the eyes.

"Yes," I said, meeting his gaze.

"Is he normally that late to pick you up?"

"Not always," I lied.

I set my bag down and found a place to sit under the big willow tree.

"I'll wait with you until he comes." Mr. Stone sat down next to me.

"Oh no, that's okay, Mr. Stone. I'm okay. Don't worry about it, please." I stood up and started looking out towards the road. "I bet he'll be here any minute now."

Just then, I saw Dad's blue station wagon pull up to the light.

"Look, he's here."

I started walking towards the curb, but instead of turning right, Dad went straight, passing my school.

"Dad!" I yelled, but he couldn't hear me.

"Come!" Mr. Stone shouted, "We'll catch up to him."

I hesitated, watching Mr. Stone get into his red truck.

"C'mon, Sam! I'll get you to him."

I jumped in the truck, and Mr. Stone sped out of the parking lot. We could see Dad in the distance, stopped at a red light. We needed to be faster to catch him. The light turned green. Dad went right, then took a quick left into a plaza where he parked.

"There! He went in there," I shouted.

Mr. Stone's face seemed to change. He looked as though he'd just heard something sad.

"Yes, I see that."

We parked next to Dad's station wagon. Mr. Stone put his hand on my shoulder before unclipping his seatbelt. "You wait here. Let me go get him."

"No, I'm okay from here. Thanks for the ride, Mr. Stone!"

I jumped out of the truck and sprinted toward the only building in the lot.

"Sam, wait!" Mr. Stone shouted.

I ignored him, hoping he'd drive away.

A big sign on the green-painted door read, "Jimmy's Hideaway Bar." I felt my heart speed up as I opened the door.

The bar was empty, except for Dad, the barman, and a guy with tattoos playing pool in the corner.

"Dad," I whispered.

Only the barman was looking at me. He tapped Dad on the shoulder. Dad lifted his head from his resting position on his hands, "What is it, Jim?"

The barman pointed at me.

As Dad turned around to see me, I heard the green door open.

"Sam, what are you doing here?"

I noticed an empty shot glass on the counter in front of him.

"You were supposed to pick him up half an hour ago."

Mr. Stone stepped in front of me, blocking my view.

"Who the hell are you?"

"Sam's tennis coach."

"Tennis?" Dad climbed off the stool.

"Mr. Stone, wait." I tried to shove ahead, but Dad was already in Mr. Stone's face.

"Your son's showing a little promise out there."

As Dad edged past him, Mr. Stone bumped against an empty pool table.

Dad looked at me with sharp, threatening eyes. "Get in the car! Now!"

I didn't hesitate, sprinting out of the bar. I noticed the time on the dashboard when I entered the station wagon. Twenty minutes later, Dad walked out of the bar, crying.

"He said they've been calling you Circus Sam." His eyes were red, and a steady stream of tears flowed.

"I just don't know how to carry on without her, Sam."

I didn't look up at Dad, but I could feel his eyes on me.

"I miss her, too." I finally said, feeling a thickness in my throat.

When I lifted my eyes to look at him, his head was flat against the steering wheel. I put my hand on his.

"Give me another chance, Sam."

I leaned over and wrapped my arms around his back.

Dad lifted off the steering wheel. I began crying as he hugged me.

"I love you, Sam."

"I love you too."

As we reversed out of the parking lot, I asked, "What did Mr. Stone say to you in there?"

He shifted the gear into park. "That I'll lose you before the 9th grade if I continue on like this."

I moved to the front of my seat. "So, I can keep playing tennis?"

"On one condition." Dad pulled his white wide-brimmed bucket hat from under the seat and placed it on my head. I studied myself in the sun-visor mirror. I looked dorky, but anything beat a face full of sunscreen.

"Only at practice," I said.

Dad nodded, extending his hand towards me.

When I shook Dad's hand, he squeezed and pulled me into his chest. We stayed like that for a few minutes, more tears dropping on my head.

About the Author

If you benefited from this book, please consider posting an online review. Thank you in advance.

South African-born author and singer-songwriter Luke Beling grew up immersed in the music of the 1960s and 1970s, influenced by the records his father played and the struggles of his native country. As a twenty-something, Beling developed a deep appreciation for subversive literature, particularly fiction that defended the outcast and celebrated the resilience of the human spirit. Beling believes that art should capture both the wonder and the hard work of life. Inspired by his travels around the world, Beling's songs and stories aim to convey profound truths and insights.

Visit the author's website at https://lukebeling.com/

Follow on social media:
Facebook: http://facebook.com/lukebelingmusic
Instagram: https://www.instagram.com/luke.beling/
X: https://x.com/BelingLuke?ref_src=twsrc%5E-google%7Ctwcamp%5Eserp%7Ctwgr%5Eauthor
Amazon: https://www.amazon.com/stores/Luke-Beling/author/B0DBY964ZV?ref=ap_rdr&isDramIntegrated=true&shoppingPortalEnabled=true
Goodreads: https://www.goodreads.com/author/show/50770398.Luke_Beling

About the Publisher

Sulis International Press publishes select fiction and nonfiction in a variety of genres under four imprints:

- Riversong Books (fiction)

- Sulis Press (general nonfiction)

- Keledei Publications (spirituality)

- Sulis Academic Press (academic works)

For more, visit the website at
https://sulisinternational.com

Subscribe to the newsletter at
https://sulisinternational.com/subscribe/

Follow on social media
https://www.facebook.com/SulisInternational
https://twitter.com/Sulis_Intl
https://www.pinterest.com/Sulis_Intl/
https://www.instagram.com/sulis_international/

www.ingramcontent.com/pod-product-compliance
Lightning Source LLC
Chambersburg PA
CBHW020831260626
47169CB00003B/933